Drops of Sunlight

A Novel by
Kristy Lee

First Published in 2022 by Blossom Spring Publishing
Drops Of Sunlight Copyright © 2022 Kristy Lee
ISBN 978-1-7396277-3-7
E: admin@blossomspringpublishing.com
W: www.blossomspringpublishing.com
Published in the United Kingdom. All rights reserved under
International Copyright Law. Contents and/or cover may
not be reproduced in whole or in part
without the express written consent of the publisher.
Names, characters, places and incidents are either products
of the author's imagination or are used fictitiously.

For Jeannie and her love of the Colorado Rockies.

A special thank you to my beta readers.
Your input is invaluable!
Rita Potter, Jean Rushing, Jeannie Lakis, and Tara DeWitt.

Love is the closest thing we have to magic – Aquamarine (film)

Prologue

May

Light is dancing through tree branches, casting shadows across my skin.

I set the empty plastic cup down beside me, swallowing the last bit of iced tea as I do.

The back of my hand gathers drops of sweat as I nervously wipe my forehead.

He'll be here. Calm down.

The anxiety of what is about to happen is heating my already overheated body.

When Dylan agreed to meet me at our boulder—the one that we carved our names into—so that we can share our first kiss, I was thrilled. No, I was *elated*. I tried to seem casual when I asked him if he had ever kissed a girl before and again when I suggested that he kiss me to get it over with. Of course, he took his sweet time in responding, staring intently at the bald eagle that was soaring in the distance, acting as though he didn't hear me. The sun was illuminating his face in an angelic aura as the fear of rejection darkened mine with dread.

I let out a much-needed breath when he finally agreed to the kiss with a simple nod, and a "sure" that was so subtle I almost missed it.

Now I sit waiting—electric anticipation, causing my skin to prickle.

This boulder is our favorite spot on the ranch because it sits high underneath the pine and aspen trees; the sunflower field is in perfect view and the white tops of the blue mountains dot the skyline in the distance.

This view is the background not only to this monumental moment, but to my entire life, sprinkling my memories with their beauty. I do not believe it is possible that there could be a more magical place in the world than this single boulder.

I chew on my fingernail as my nerves get the best of me. Dylan and I have been the best of friends since we were six years old, our relationship never being more than childhood innocence until a single moment that changed everything.

Two months ago—May sixteenth to be exact—was the day my family and I arrived at the mountain for the summer. Dylan was waiting for me on the front porch like he always does. He had on a loose gray t-shirt and his raven hair was pushed back off his forehead.

I had never consciously paid attention to his face before, even though I knew it better than my own. But on this particular day, I suddenly became very aware of its details. Maybe it was because I was older, maybe it was because of the way his shirt fluttered in the warm breeze as I ran to embrace him, or maybe it was the fact that I had started thinking about boys in a way I never had before, but for the first time I saw—I mean *really* saw him. The deep dimple in his cheek when he smiled wide, the gap in his two front teeth, the faint dusting of freckles running across the bridge of his nose.

I noticed when I wrapped my arms around him, that for the first time in our lives, he was taller than me. I was forced to stand on the tips of my toes for our embrace. His cheek brushed mine softly when I released him from my death grip causing my heart to inexplicably jump, bouncing off my ribcage as it did.

It has been one month since that fateful day, and I have spent the time since becoming more and more infatuated with everything about him. I find the way he calls sandwiches 'sammies' nauseatingly adorable, the sprinkling of hair on his skinny arms beautiful, and I even find the shaking in his changing voice to be magical.

My favorite thing about him, though, is his big, brown eyes. The best way I can think to describe them is that they are the exact same shade as the maple leaves that fall back home in Vermont. You know when autumn first hits and the leaves drift to the ground and after a couple of days their orange and red colors begin to darken? I asked my mom once what that color was called and she said, "burnt sienna." As an interior decorator, she is great with colors, so I trust her.

While those eyes are my favorite thing, his sense of humor is a close second. My sides always ache, and my mouth goes wide with silent laughter whenever he does his impression of Henry, his mom's cigar-smoking ranch hand that swears in every sentence.

Now the moment has come where our relationship will change forever, a shift will occur in the universe and our future will forge a new path as a result.

Kissing your best friend is a big deal and while I am excited to the point of giddy, my heart senses a feeling of dread. Truthfully, I'm afraid—afraid to lose my oldest and dearest friend. As I sit on this boulder, emersed in these thoughts, it takes me a moment to notice the blurry figure dipping over the hill. The familiarity of the body running towards me lets me know that it's him.

Suddenly the fear building in my chest evaporates and all I can think is *Yes*.

I shake as I wipe my mouth to prepare it for my mom's strawberry-flavored Chapstick. I have no idea what boys like when kissing, but she is always putting this stuff on, so I thought I should too. I rub my lips together, noticing the slight taste of muted strawberry.

I cannot believe I am about to have my first kiss.

Finally, I am growing up.

Dylan is gleaming with sweat as he takes a labored breath beside me. Even his sweat smells good. *God*, boys are the best.

"Sorry I'm late. Had to feed the horses." He says this while wiping his palms against the fabric of his jeans. Maybe he is just as nervous for this as I am.

"No prob'."

"Ready?" Dylan looks at everything but me as he chews on his bottom lip and I have to resist the urge to hug him and tell him it will all be okay.

I shrug, desperate to seem cool. "Sure."

I beg my heart to calm down when I angle my body to face him, worried that he can see its rhythmic pounding through the skin on my chest. As I turn my body, the strap of my yellow tank top falls down, revealing my collarbone. Dylan's eyes glance nervously towards the skin between my neck and shoulder, and he takes in what he sees with intensity. It is as though he is trying to take a mental picture of something he's not sure he will ever see again. My skin blushes in response.

"Should I just do it?" He asks this as his eyes finally meet mine, making me grateful that I'm sitting down for fear I would topple over.

"I guess so."

Dylan leans in slowly, he licks his lips and bats his eyelashes as he does, clearly unsure of what to do. I can no longer wait—the anxiety is killing me, so I quickly plant my mouth on his.

After a beat, we break to breathe. I run my fingertips over my mouth, relieved at how lovely his lips felt on mine.

"How was it?" The crease between his brows causes me to wonder if it was not as nice for him as it was for me.

"Okay, I guess." I lie, it was *marvelous*.

"Should I try it with tongue?"

Oh. Maybe he didn't hate it. "'Kay."

Dylan leans in and tentatively places his tongue in my mouth. He tastes of minty toothpaste and its deliciousness is unparalleled.

A nervous minute later, we stop so I can check the time on his watch, "I have to go, my parents told me to come back right away. I'll call you after dinner." My heart is beating so hard I am certain he can hear it.

"Yeah—no prob. Hey, May, can we do that again sometime?"

"We can do that forever, Dylan."

And I meant it.

Chapter One

Miranda
Six Years and Ten Months Later

When the door creaks open, dust tumbles down from above, shimmering against the morning sun.

I take a deep breath, the familiar smell striking a nerve.

I cannot believe I am back here.

I walk in, dropping my suitcase on the faded red rug, causing plumes of dust to fly up. I cough as I make a mental note to add rug cleaning to my list of chores. The task before me is not going to be an easy one, I have just two weeks to get this dump livable before my mother shows up with the summer tenants. I might be in over my head with this project, but thanks to the mistakes I have made, I do not have much of a choice.

The sad thing is that when I was a child, it would have been unfathomable that I would ever call this place a dump. This realization causes a lump to form in my throat, the ache for the past lodges itself against my spine.

When I was growing up, I spent many summers here, weaving through the trees with the breeze at my back, but it was different then—*I* was different then. My parents were still together, and I was naïve, believing that this home and this mountain was something magical. Now, through the eyes of a bitter twenty-year-old, it barely passes as livable.

I step behind the couch, careful not to touch the cream-colored vase on the oak side table, to open the curtains framing the large living room window. I turn my face to the side as I do, to avoid inhaling dust again.

Despite my bitterness at being here, the view still manages to take my breath away.

It is early in the day, so the sun is low. Low enough for its rays to beam in though the tree branches, creating halos around their pine needles. The mountains peak through the breaks in the trees, with their white tops and bluish tint creating a heavy contrast to the thick coffee-colored tree trunks and sparse forest floor. Up high in the Rocky Mountains, the forest floor is mostly just some shrubbery and lots of fallen and browning needles.

The image displayed before me is branded into my mind's eye and etched across the ridges of my brain. It plays like a soft record to all my childhood memories.

I probably know this view better than I know my own face and it is because of this view—and this view alone—that makes renting this dilapidated home worth the extravagant price.

I exhale a weighty breath and wipe off the dust that has collected on my shoulders. No time to reminisce, I have a lot of work to do and better get to it.

This place is spotless.

Well, as spotless as an outdated falling apart home can be. This is the type of place that looks nice as long as you do not look at it too closely. Its beauty is a façade and will fade once it reveals its true, ugly self, just as it did in my childhood.

I have outdone myself and shined up this rusty trash can and, as a bonus, seven days of nonstop cleaning has proven cathartic.

I only thought about my ex twice and only cried once.
Go me.

For years, it was just me and my parents who used this home during the summers. It was a lovely getaway from the busy work-obsessed lives of my parents and a place I came to love from the age of six to fourteen. In the years since my parents divorced and I stopped coming here, it has mostly been shuttered up and unused. There have only been a couple times over the years that my mother has found someone who wants to spend a lot of money to stay here during the summer. It does not happen often, though, because my mom likes to stay in the house with the renters so that she can be here to provide them with whatever they need and keep an eye on them. It is sort of like a long-term bed and breakfast situation except without the breakfast. She claims it is hard for her to get away from work like that now, but I know it is because it's not the same for her to come here without my dad. When she and my dad did it, they made it seem easy.

Now, since I am *very* available, my parents think this is a great opportunity for me to be the one to babysit the family wanting to spend eight weeks here.

I shove the vacuum into the already stuffed closet underneath the staircase. To get the door to shut over the overpouring of cleaning supplies, I have to use all my strength, only to then crumble to the floor overcome with exhaustion. The buckling wood planks scrape my knee as I do.

The freshly wiped down glass inlay on the gray cabinet across from me is kind enough to show me my reflection.

Wow, I look like a garbage troll.

My unwashed hair and dirt-smudged face frame tired, red eyes that seem to be glowing like I am some kind of villain in a horror film. I run my hand into the tangled mess on my head in a failed attempt to fix it.

An exhausted sigh escapes my mouth. *I should probably get cleaned up.* Heck, when was the last time I took a shower? Have I even taken one since I got here?

Yikes, I must be more depressed than I thought.

Oh well, I don't really care what I look like. These tenants will have just to deal with the fact they will be sharing a summer home in the mountains with a child of *Deliverance*, maybe it will add to the rustic charm they are seeking.

The old red Subaru is great for this type of terrain because getting down to the small town at the foot of this steep mountain can be quite the ordeal, thanks to the unpaved and winding roads. Even after two hundred thousand miles, rusted paint, and a door handle on the passenger side that doesn't work, this car still handles the terrain like a champ. My parents left this car with the house so I was not sure it would even start thanks to the couple of years of no one driving it, but after a few attempts, it did. I was relieved because it is the only reliable mode of transportation I have. When I drove here, I had parked my little Volkswagen Beetle in the garage the day I arrived, knowing I wouldn't drive it again until I left at the end of the summer. It's not exactly designed for these roads.

The car is bumping along, forcing me to grip the steering wheel—my knuckles turning white. I look up to the rearview mirror and my hair still looks like a matted rat's nest. I had opted for sleep instead of a shower last night and it shows. I tried to sweep my tawny-colored locks up into a bun but that only seemed to have made it worse.

The sad thing is that I used to take great pride in my appearance, spending an hour each morning doing my makeup and fixing my hair. Now, I am not even sure where my makeup is or if I even brought it with me. What's the point? I am not here to impress anyone. A sudden thought bubbles into my mind before I can stop it—*I just hope Dylan doesn't see me like this*—but I quickly brush it away.

I stop and park at the small grocery store, keeping the engine running, so that the air conditioning can blow for a few moments more. It is surprisingly hot today, usually May in the mountains is still fairly cool.

As the chilled air blasts across my face, I get lost in my head and my nerves start to build as I ponder who the tenants are that will be living with me. I do not know anything about them—they could be murderers or thieves or something. *How could my parents do this to me?* I know I messed up and taking care of this place for the summer might have been the wrong choice, but I reassure myself that spending six weeks in a rehab facility without any freedom would be way worse.

The engine shuts off, sputtering a bit as it does, reminding me that mom said I need to take it in at some point for an oil change. The groan that the door makes as I finally open it makes me jump unexpectedly causing the middle-aged woman jogging by to give me a strange expression. Embarrassed, I quickly make my way into the little corner store that *literally* sits on a corner and is called *The Corner Mart*.

This town is too small to care about being creative and tends to stick to the obvious. *The Gas Station, The Clothing Store,* and *The Horse Feed Store* are just a few of the original gems this place showcases.

The front door to *The Corner Mart* dings a bell when I push it open, but other than that, there is an eerie silence that fills the space. There are just five rows of food so you can see the entire store as you walk in. I immediately spot two other people shopping, silently pushing their shopping carts as they do. The store owner—a man whose name I cannot recall—is not even playing background music like most grocery stores do. Grabbing the nearest cart, I pull out the list my mom emailed this morning, forcing the scary movie vibe of this place out of my head.

Just as the word *milk* enters my field of vision, a voice startles me, "May?" I turn abruptly—who the heck said that? "Hey, it's you."

I do not say anything, but I know instantly who is standing in front of me. My heart freezes, the blood in its chambers stops flowing. For the first time in my life, I'm completely speechless.

"It's Dylan. Dylan Ryder. Your next-door neighbor? We grew up together? I haven't seen you in at least six years—almost seven. How the hell are ya?" I can tell by his tone that he is being ornery, he knows he does not need to explain to me who he is, but I guess this is the game we are playing right now.

My eyes drift up and down the length of the body in front of me. He looks so . . . so . . . different. The once gawky kid with scraped knees and a gap in his front teeth is long gone and in his place was a tall, clearly fit, bronzed, and dare I say, God of a man. The only thing that is exactly as it was, is his eyes. He still has those same eyes, the same ones that once made my heart soar. Dylan has brown eyes and I'm not even a huge fan of brown eyes. Neither of my past boyfriends had them and I have never gone out of my way to admire a pair, but Dylan's are different. There is nothing ordinary or common about them. My mother once described the color to me as burnt sienna. They remind me of fallen leaves in autumn and I can't help but think of him whenever I'm home in Vermont and the seasons change causing the ground to become coated in a layer of darkened maple leaves.

He boars into me waiting for a response, forcing me to quickly regain my composure from the initial shock of him. I straighten my shoulders and square my jaw as annoyance rips through me. He is the *last* person on planet earth I want to see right now. Just *great*.

My anxiety is off the charts but I must force myself to seem indifferent. "Um, yeah. I remember you. Kinda. I guess it's been a while." I am very aware of my appearance right now which makes me wish I could crawl into a hole and die.

"Why're you here? My mom said you were at college, I just figured I'd never see you again." I catch a hint of *something* in his voice as he says this. Something similar to how I am feeling right now—annoyed.

"I *am* in college; I'm just here helping my mother out with the tenants for the summer. I go back to Alfred University in August." The lie comes out without a second thought. *What is wrong with me?* My pathetic quota has surpassed its limit for today.

"Oh cool, I'm just here for the summer, too. I come every summer, though. I love it here."

"You in college?" I ask this with a snarky tone, knowing he was never the college type with his muddy boots and passion for being outside. I used to think he was allergic to the insides of buildings.

"Um, no. I work on the ranch here in the summers and in the winters, I'm back home in Boulder helping my grandpa with his store."

Dylan tucks his fist into the pocket of his well-fitting jeans, and I can't help but notice the muscle of his arm flex as he does. Could this moment get any worse?

"Okay, well cool. See you later then," I say as I turn away abruptly, desperate for this hellfire to end.

"Okay, later, May." No one has called me May since I

dropped the nickname when I was fourteen and decided I was too cool for the dorky moniker Dylan came up with all those years ago.

"It's Miranda now." The snarky way I spit this out startles even me.

"Oh okay, sorry." Dylan offers a lopsided grin, and I can tell he is mocking me.

Ass.

Chapter Two

Dylan

Finally, I have arrived. Rusty—my mom's latest sheepdog, greets me as I come through the gate in my favorite red pickup truck.

It's early and the sun is just now rising over the tops of the trees. I drove all night to get here as quickly as possible—flying out the door of the store right at closing time.

Every year I impatiently wait to head back up to the ranch. This has always been my favorite place. Most of my memories here are awesome: the smell of the pine, the horseback riding, the sunflower field, the adventures with May. Not all my memories are great, though, namely the one of May never speaking to me again after we kissed for the first, and last, time. I have tried to push down the thoughts of losing my best friend to a simple kiss, regretting that it ever happened. If I had known then that she would never speak to me again, I would never have done it.

After six years of not hearing from her, I have finally accepted the death of our friendship but memories of her still flash in my mind, especially when I'm here. So many of my childhood memories have her in them that it is almost impossible for me not to think of her.

I bet she never thinks of me, though. She has not stepped foot on this mountain since that fateful day, and, according to her very vain social media accounts, we have nothing in common anymore.

"Dylan, finally! I'm so glad you're here, son!"

"Hey, Mom," I say as she throws her thin arms around me. Odd, it seems like she has lost weight by the feel of her ribs when I squeeze my arms around her. I brush the thought aside, too happy to be here to think of much else.

"I know you just got up here, but can you head back down the mountain to get groceries? I'm really behind; Dave went back home early this year, so I've been without my ranch hand for almost a week now." Mom has been through many ranch hands; they are not the most reliable kind.

"Sure, no problem. Just get me a list."

The small corner grocery store is surprisingly well stocked. I can usually get everything I need for at least two weeks' worth of meals so that we do not have to constantly make the forty-five-minute drive back down the mountain.

"Glad to see you're back, Dylan, I was wonderin' when you'd hit town." Old Freddy has owned this store for the last thirty years and says this exact sentence to me every spring. It has become a kind of tradition for me to come in for my yearly greeting from him.

"Hey Freddy, it's great to see you too, man."

"Did you hear the Carlson kid is back?"

WHAT. My heart stops, then sputters back to life.

"Oh? Really? Who told you that?" I say this as nonchalantly as possible, but my voice comes out louder than I intend.

"My sister saw her drivin' into town 'bout a week ago. Said she was headed up the mountain."

"Well, I didn't know that, but I don't really talk to her anymore, so it doesn't matter much to me."

"Uh-hmmm." I do not appreciate the sarcastic doubt from Freddy, so I grab a shopping cart and get to it.

I am through the list quickly, a benefit to having shopped here my entire life is knowing exactly where any ingredient is in this small store, and just as I walk by the ice cream, the bell dings, causing me to look up.

This town is small, *too* small. Everybody knows everybody, so if I see someone I do not immediately recognize, as a resident of this small town, I cannot help but be curious. It's a woman and she appears young and slightly disheveled, like she just rolled out of bed.

I glance over to Freddy, and he gives me the eyebrow raised 'oh crap' face and my stomach does a summersault, tumbling all the way down to the soles of my feet.

May.

I would recognize that face anywhere, its long lashes and sky-blue eyes haunting me for most of my life. My first thought is to flee, but it would be so weird if I left this store without saying hello to her. It would also add fuel to the rumor mill fire and the last thing I want to do is give Freddy something to gossip about. If anything is going on in this place, he is sure to inform every living soul of it.

I approach quietly and carefully, plotting each step in her direction as though that will somehow make this interaction any less horrendous.

"May?"

She turns and looks at me with the snarliest face I have ever seen, instant regret filling my now very turbulent stomach.

"Hey, it's you." I force myself to say, only to hear crickets in return. I continue, "It's Dylan. Dylan Ryder. Your next-door neighbor? We grew up together? I haven't seen you in at least six years—almost seven. How the hell are ya?" Is she seriously pretending not to recognize me? Is this a joke?

Her eyes drift up and down the length me, sizing me up like a hog at auction. I take the opportunity to do the same, noticing her sweatpants and stained oversized t-shirt. While I cannot really see her body, I can see her face and it looks the same as it always has. She clearly is not wearing any makeup and for a moment I am taken aback by how young she looks.

"Um, yeah. I remember you. Kinda. I guess it's been a while." *Kinda*?

"Why're you here? My mom said you were at college, I just figured I'd never see you again." I know why she is here. I know that her mom's house is going to be occupied with tenants for eight weeks, and I even know who the tenants are, but I never imagined they would send May to take care of this. A large lump forms just below my Adam's apple. The ensuing awkwardness of this summer has become painfully apparent.

"I *am* in college; I'm just here helping my mother out with the tenants for the summer. I go back to Alfred University in August." Oh, I get it, she thinks she is too good for the likes of me.

"Oh cool, I'm just here for the summer, too. I come every summer, though. I love it here."

As we exchange small talk, I take the opportunity to observe her. Even though it has been so long since I have seen her in person, she still looks the same. Unfortunately, her face is just as beautiful as ever, in fact more so, which makes my stomach drop the same way it does whenever I have food poisoning. The few times I checked her out over the years on her social media pages told me she was still gorgeous, but I secretly hoped that was thanks to filters and photoshopping.

As I gaze into her bright eyes, I realize it was wishful thinking, and when she tucks a piece of her golden-brown hair behind her ears, I am transported back to the windy days on the ranch when I used to watch that same hair blow in the breeze.

"I bet I can beat you to that tree." May says this while leaning into a position, ready to run even though I haven't agreed to anything yet.

"No way. I'm way faster than…" She bolts and is already two feet ahead of me before I even have the chance to start. I yell "cheater!" but my voice is drowned out by our shared laughter as we race through the sunflowers toward the finish line.

I don't usually let May win at anything because we are both so competitive that it does not even occur to me to do that. Today, though, I am enjoying the view too much to pull ahead of her, loving how her long hair is blowing back behind her and how the sun is shining down, framing her in a soft glow.

"You in college?" May's snarky tone drags me back to the present, kicking and screaming. Her face is twisted with disgust and she is looking at me like I'm a bug crawling up her precious forearm.

After a painful few more seconds of small talk, she ends the torment of this moment. "Okay, well cool. See you later then."

I shrug, trying not to appear bothered by the sight of her, "Okay, later, May."

"It's Miranda now." Oh, *brother.*

"Oh okay, sorry."

Get me the heck out of this store.

Chapter Three

Miranda

Dawn breaks and the sun is shining through the window directly into my eyes forcing me awake.

My back aches as I lean forward to stretch—the flower pattern of the fabric on the reclining chair leaving slight indentations on my arm.

After seeing Dylan yesterday, I crumbled into the old and faded piece of furniture in the living room and dreamt of our childhood. The starry nights, the laughs, the afternoons spent running through the sunflower field and climbing trees flood back into my consciousness like a freight train. The memories play on a screen in my mind, almost as if I am watching someone else's story.

Through the flickering images of brown eyes, dimples, bruised knees, and sticky fingers covered in melted ice cream, one image keeps trying to force its way to the forefront. It's the same one that I have spent the last seven years desperate to forget. The last time I saw Dylan—the last time I was in these mountains. I was only fourteen years old and had just had the most thrilling first kiss when I walked into this very house to my waiting parents.

I do not remember much about how the conversation went; their voices became muffled after I heard the word 'divorce.'

I bet most people do not know the exact moment they lost their childhood naiveté, but there was one. There was a single moment in your life where it all changed and shifted you from an innocent child to something else—something real and devoid of the magic that only comes with youth. I know that exact moment and it happened right here in this living room as my parents shattered my world. It was after I spent one last glorious and carefree summer with Dylan and only minutes after I sat with him on that boulder overlooking the sunflowers.

I was still basking in the glow that emanated from my lips when my parents' declaration turned that glow inky black and sticky with pain.

That moment changed the projection of my life. I no longer had this unwavering belief in fairy tales, magic, or love. The stark realization made it hard for me to care—about any of it. How could I care about this life if it was empty of the magic I used to believe in? The only way I was able to move forward was to focus on other things—like having fun and forgetting other things—like Dylan.

Dylan represented my past self, the one who was blinded to reality. The time I spent running through the sunflowers, pulling Dylan by the hand while drops of sunlight fell all around us began to fade into the background of my now bitter heart and it was that bitterness that gave me the strength to never speak to Dylan again.

Dylan tried. *Man*, did he try.

He called over and over and wrote numerous letters, but I ghosted him completely, never once bothering to call him back or read a single word he wrote. After a while, my mother stopped trying to give me letters from him and the phone stopped ringing. He drifted into the background until he eventually faded out of my life completely.

To help me cope with losing him, and myself, I became convinced that he was just a simple childhood friend and we were always destined to grow apart. I even began to think that he was never really that cute and I was too cool for him. I know it sounds cold, and I guess it really was, but it was the only way I could let him go at the time.

Now, almost seven years and one gloriously failed attempt at college later, I am right back in the place where it all started. What's worse about this entire catastrophe that is my life is that I was so *together*. I had it all. At least, that's what everyone thought. The truth is that I was living two lives, the one everyone saw and then the one in my head. The Miranda everyone knew was happy, popular, and had the world at her fingertips. The Miranda in my head felt like the world's best actress. I forced myself to appear happy, but the second I was alone, that illusion drained from my body and all that was left was an empty shell. Even with this truth though, I never imagined I would be kicked out of college and staring into the face of a furrow-browed judge telling me that I need to get help. He told my parents to consider rehab and when he used the word 'addict' my chest began to cave in on itself. After successfully getting my DUI dropped to a reckless driving charge and my parents forking over a hefty sum to pay my fines, I get to have the pleasure of "working it off" this summer. It was either that or to agree to a stint in rehab, so here I am.

Here is what I know: the judge was wrong—I do not have a drinking problem. What I have is a life problem. While I recognize that I'm depressed and have been for some time, I know that I should not be here. I would rather continue to pretend to be happy as long as that means I'm in college, at a party, being glamorous and talking to some guy who plays on the football team, but instead, I'm stuck in this hell that I have created. Without any money, a degree, or a job, I am left with zero options but to obey my parents' wishes.

I was surprised that my parents offered me the summer home over rehab, I guess they think fresh air will cure all my problems, but they always think ridiculous things like that. To make matters worse, the embarrassment and shame of what I have become have spiraled me into an even deeper depression than I was already in.

However, the idea of my parents sitting at the kitchen table, forced to discuss the problem of me, makes me laugh almost sadistically. They have avoided each other almost completely since the divorce, so in a twisted way I am happy to know they are talking again, even if it is over the failure that is their daughter. In a deeper more vulnerable way, I even hope that they might reconcile and we could be a family again.

I shake the thought from my head and rub the sleep from my eyes. I just need to get through this summer working off my debt and show my parents that I'm not an alcoholic so that I can be free to move on with my life.

I know the time here will be awkward. Heck, I knew that I would come across Dylan at some point. Our houses are too close to each other and this mountain is too small not to. I should have been more prepared for our encounter yesterday, and now, I'm bothered with wondering why I wasn't.

Just then and much to my surprise, a dark thought creeps into the back of my head settling against the base of my neck: *man, I need a drink.*

I spend the rest of the afternoon trying to distract myself from the wine I know is sitting in the cellar by cooking, cleaning, and re-washing all the sheets, but the thought of it is still lingering.

After convincing myself that, *one drink is fine,* and, *I am not actually an addict; I just like a drink now and then. It's not a big deal,* I give up the fight and head towards the cellar.

I should not be going near this wine. I know that. After my parents argued with me for an hour and half about if they should leave the wine here or not, I was able to convince them that I would not touch it. My mom only ultimately agreed to leave it because she wants the guests to have access to it as part of her hospitality package and only after I made promises that I thought I could keep at the time.

I was passionate with my speech, "I know you're worried about my drinking, but I promise you I won't touch it. I'll drive myself to rehab if I can't stay away from it. I *swear*. You know how many bottles you have; you can come and count them at the end of the summer. I'm only twenty, it's not like I can buy more to replace them. The only times I have drank before was when someone else brought alcohol to a party. I don't have that big of a drinking problem, let me use this as a chance to prove it to you."

"Lynn, I think we should leave it. Alcohol is always going to be around. She needs to learn to stay away from it. We can't keep it from her forever. Let's give her this chance to show us she's not an addict like she says."

"I don't like it, but I guess you're right. This is your one chance, Miranda, if I find out you have had any of that wine, you're going to rehab. I'll be checking it when I bring the tenants."

"Don't make us regret this." When my father said this to me, I believed that I would be able to stay away from it without it being a problem at all. Now as I walk down the rickety steps, I ignore the pang of guilt and shame that washes over me.

Rain dops pour on the tin roof of this old home, creating a soft musical sound. I'm resting my chin on the back of my trusty flower-patterned chair, watching as the day turns to night. The darkening clouds lull me into a lazy drunken sleep.

Something is *ringing*.

It keeps on—*Ring, ring, ring.*

I slowly drift back from the depths of my dreamless sleep to awaken to some awful noise created by the demons of hell.

It takes me a moment to recognize it as the doorbell. I fall out of the chair and peek out the window to see who it is.

Dylan.

Crap. And, of course, I look even more wretched than I did when I saw him yesterday.

"What do you want?" I bellow like the wench that I have become.

"Wow, you sound so pleasant."

"Seriously Dylan, I don't have time for this."

"What're you so busy doin'?" I open the door a creak and see his raised right eyebrow displaying his sarcasm. The rain has stopped and the sunset is peaking through broken clouds.

". . . Napping."

Dylan rolls his eyes and reaches his hand out.

"What's this?"

"My mom made me come drop this off. It's mail that was accidentally delivered to the ranch. It happens sometimes."

"Oh, whatever. Is that it?"

"Of course, trust me, I'm not here to see you."

"Good."

"Good."

Dylan saunters off, hands in pockets. The muscles on

his back and shoulders are visible through the thin fabric of his white t-shirt and so I quickly slam the door shut, not wanting to dwell too long on his backside.

I really need to get a grip. It must be hormones. I haven't had sex in months ever since what's-his-face dumped me at a party in front of all my friends and I stormed off in his car, totaling it.

As I lean back against the door, running my hands over my face trying to force the painful memories away, I hear a quiet knock so I creak the door open again.

"What now?"

"Look, my mom will be ticked if you don't come to dinner tonight. She insisted I invite you and she won't get off my back about it. Can you just come and get it over with? You don't have to talk to me."

"Ugh. Fine," I say this with the annoyance of a child, "I will, but only because I haven't seen your mom in years and my mom would kill me if she thought I was rude to yours."

"It'll be ready in an hour."

"Fine."

"Fine."

The orange hues of the setting sun strike Dylan's eyes as he turns to leave, emphasizing their velvety hue. That is the one thing I have never been able to forget about him—those eyes.

I *must* redeem my appearance.

I clean myself up, drink two cups of coffee and a Gatorade before I am finally ready for this dinner.

As I gaze at the girl in the mirror, I must say, I look *good*.

The form fitting t-shirt and curve loving jeans appear casual but were, in fact, intricately planned. The light blush on my cheeks and loosely formed braid are both sexy and sweet. A deadly combination.

I walk the short distance to the Ryder ranch under a big bright moon. A wash of moonlight sprinkles over the treetops, teasing their beauty. The Ryder ranch has always been special to me. An enchanting place with horses and sheep and plenty of barns to play hide and seek in. As I walk up the path, memories spent here with Dylan flood from the depths of my soul and crash into my consciousness causing my heart to ache.

I should have had one more drink before coming here.

The thought enters my mind before I even have a chance to stop it. I shake my head in frustration as I see Mrs. Ryder swing the large wooden door open, her beautiful long black hair still just as it has always been, except now with a few gray hairs sweeping through.

"May! I can't believe it! It's been too long, dear!" She says this as she wraps me in a bear hug, the smell of thyme on her skin.

"Hey, Mrs. Ryder. It's so nice to see you, too." I do not bother to correct her; I admire Dylan's mom too much to ever tell her I no longer go by that name.

"Please come in. We're having chicken. I'm so happy you've joined us. We've missed you up here. The mountain hasn't been the same since you stopped coming." As Mrs. Ryder turns back toward the house, I notice something off, she seems skinnier than I remember and there is a slight gray cast over her skin. It has been a long time so it may just a normal part of aging, but something about it strikes me as odd.

I follow her inside, ignoring her comments about missing me, and notice immediately that this place has not changed one bit. The furniture, the smell of wood, the sound of the fire crackling transports me back in time in an instant.

The Ryder's home is truly one of beauty. Its walls are made from the trunks of large pine trees and in the center of the large living room space there is a built-in stone fireplace that stretches wider than my Volkswagen. The floors are a beautiful dark hardwood with a few strategically placed rugs. It houses some of the classic aspects of a typical Colorado home, including several sets of antlers and two bear fur rugs that were here when the Ryders bought the place. The open living room space has a large and also open kitchen attached to it with granite countertops and more cabinets than I would know what to do with. Their home puts ours to shame. I think about our boring, standard, ready-made house that lacks any trace of originality and shake my head with envy. Dylan once told me that his parents invested their life savings into remodeling it and before my parents divorced, they were inspired by the Ryder home and planned to remodel ours. Of course, without my dad, my mom no longer sees the point.

Dylan strides in from the kitchen wearing the same outfit he had on from earlier, instantly causing my mind, and heart, to shutter. Every time I have seen him since I got back, I become more *aware* of everything about him. The way he holds his shoulders and how broad they are; how he has more hair along the length of his arms then he did when we were kids making me wonder where else he has hair; the way his legs move with long, smooth strides. When we were kids, I also noticed everything about him but when I noticed him at fourteen, I thought he was adorable and cute and kissable. Now, my thoughts still turn to kissing, but also of something else. Need pools low in my belly, causing my thighs to clench.

This . . . is new.

His hair is messy but I can tell it's intentionally styled that way. He is freshly clean-shaven—the whisper of a shadow that I saw earlier is gone and I wonder if he shaved to try to look good for me. Not that he needs to do much to look good. As he leans against the staircase banister and Mrs. Ryder rattles on about dinner, their horses, and again about how much she has missed me coming here in the summers, Dylan remains silent. I try to engage in conversation with Mrs. Ryder but find myself barely able to pay attention as my thoughts and eyes keep lingering over to Dylan's face and body. The only movement he makes is to give me a brief and subtle once over. His clenched jaw reassures me that I succeeded in my ploy to look good.

Oh no, why do I care so much if Dylan thinks I look good? I swat away the startling thought quickly and focus on getting through this.

Dinner is *awkward*.

Mrs. Ryder never stops talking and Dylan never starts. He intentionally avoids all eye contact with me, and I have never felt more invisible in my entire life.

"So, how's college been, dear? I called and asked your mother how you're doin' but she didn't really say much." Something about the way she says this, while not making eye contact, causes my spidey-senses to tingle. I mentally scream at my mother for sharing with Mrs. Ryder what a loser I am. The last person I would want knowing is her, well, her and Dylan. I glance up to him to gauge his reaction. Does he know I lied to him at the grocery store? He is too busy pushing a carrot around his plate to seem to even hear the conversation.

"Oh, uh, it's been great. I go back in the fall. I've been doing good." I feel terrible lying about this to her, but yet, it doesn't stop the lies from spilling out.

"That's wonderful to hear, I wish Dylan could have gone to college, but oh well."

"Mom, please." For the first time since this hellish dinner began, he speaks.

"Oh okay, okay. I'm just saying it would've been nice for you to have a back-up plan in case this ranch ever went under."

"It's not ever going under, Mom. I'll make sure of it." When he says this, I notice for the first time the most significant change to his body and voice since we were kids: his confidence. He leans back in his chair, no longer with the posture of a teenager who doesn't know what to do with himself. Inexplicably, I feel my cheeks heat.

Mrs. Ryder sighs, "I know you think that Dylan, and I'm sure you're right. I just worry about how you'll manage once I'm gone. It's no joke keeping this place operating. I have confidence in your abilities, Dyl, I just wish you had a back-up plan in case something happens that's out of your control."

"Well, I don't. This ranch is my first and only plan. I have no other plans. Luckily, you aren't goin' anywhere anytime soon so we don't need to worry about it right now."

Mrs. Ryder drops her fork and lets out a huff, "I have to clean up the kitchen, can you walk May home?" I feel awkward witnessing this private conversation, which causes sadness to dip low in my stomach, reminding me that at one time, it would've been normal for me to be a part of this—a part of their family.

Dylan rolls his eyes in response and grumbles, "She'll be fine. It's not far."

"Dylan."

"Ugh. Fine. Let's go."

We both get up at the same time from the dinner table, startling the dog who jumps to his feet. I turn quickly and walk out the front door instead of bothering to wait for Dylan, yelling behind me a quick "Thanks again" to Mrs. Ryder.

Dylan falls in step behind me and even though he is quiet I can feel his presence. In fact, my body has never been more acutely aware of a person. I face forward while the cells in my body are pulling me backward, as though they are desperate to be near him. Caving to their wishes, I slow my steps to allow him to fall in line with me.

The sky is black but the stars are bright. The air is crisp and it fills my lungs with a coolness that warms my heart with more memories. The cool nighttime air is one of my favorite things about being up in the mountains. No matter how warm it was during the day; the air inevitably chills once the sun sets.

My body shivers slightly. I hope Dylan does not notice. I do not want him to think I'm an idiot for not bringing long sleeves to walk home in. He used to get so annoyed with me for that when we were kids because I would always be unprepared for the cold when the sun would start to go down—and he would be forced to give me his hoodie.

"Are you shivering?"
"No."
"May, why don't you ever remember to bring a sweater? You know it gets cold when the sun sets."
"I dunno' I just forget I guess." That's not really true. I never remember to bring a sweater because I know that no matter what, Dylan will always give me his hoodie to wear. He is always taking care of me like that.

As with any tenacious twelve-year-old boy though, he likes to complain about it. "Here, take this. You need to bring your own next time. I'm not going to keep letting you use mine." He hands me the soft gray hoodie with a dinosaur printed on the front—a T-Rex according to Dylan, and I smile.

We are walking back to the ranch after spending the afternoon climbing our favorite climbing tree and the sun is almost set behind the horizon. Our parents never worry too much about us running around the ranch, but they have one rule: be back to one of our houses before dark. Dyl has learned to know exactly when that will be, and always makes sure we do as we're told. He is the responsible one—the caretaker. While I am the one who falls asleep in the sunflowers, free from worry thanks to my never-ending trust in him.

The memory startles me a bit.

Before today, I had pushed that old carefree feeling down into the depths of my soul. A sharp pain shoots through my chest as I'm reminded that I have not felt that way since I left this place but right now, right at this very second, I can almost feel a whisper of it. I want to believe that is because I am back here on this mountain but a deeper part of me knows it is because I am near Dylan again.

Dylan walks beside me with his head lifted towards the stars. I use this opportunity to sneakily examine him. The starlight traces his face, running softly along his sharp jaw line and cupid's bow. I can see his dimple slightly but it is mostly hidden from me because he's not smiling.

A disturbing thought crosses my mind: *I have missed that freaking dimple. A lot.*

My eyes drift to his and his dark lashes bat a few times

as he continues to look up. His blatant expression of awe at the night sky creates a strange thought to flicker into my mind, *I wish he looked at me the way he looks at the stars.*

I shake in dismay at where my head is at and he notices the abrupt movement.

"What?" Somehow, in the dark, his voice sounds deeper than it did earlier.

"Nothin'." This comes out more forcefully than I intend.

We keep walking along the path and my awkwardness has now created a pathetic need to fill the silence, so I jump in, "Thanks for dinner."

"It was my mom. I had nothin' to do with it."

"Oh, yeah, I know. I just mean. . . well, thanks anyway." Wow, I sound stupid.

"Whatever." Dylan's attitude towards me turns my ears red. Now I am embarrassed and pissed so instead of shutting up, I keep talking.

"Are you mad at me for something, Dylan?" Oh my god, I have no control over my mouth anymore.

Dylan stops dead in his tracks, fisting his hands into the pockets of his jeans as he lets out an irritated sigh. "Are you kidding me?"

"No." Well, yes, sort of. I know exactly why he is mad at me but like the mature adult that I am, I choose to play this game with him.

Without blinking, Dylan goes in for the attack, "You're one of the meanest, most self-absorbed people I've ever met."

"What? No, I'm not." Does he *really* think that? I'm not that bad. *Right?*

"Whatever, I see your social media pages, I see how you are."

"Why, because I post pictures of myself? That does

not mean I'm self-absorbed. People do that, Dylan, post pictures, that's normal. Why're you creeping on my accounts, anyway?"

"Oh, get over yourself, it was one time and I wanted to see how you were since you don't speak to me anymore."

"Is this all about when we were fourteen?" I really need to learn when to shut up.

"No, I don't care about that anymore." This is the angriest I have ever seen Dylan and it suddenly occurs to me that I *really* don't care for it.

"You're not still obsessed with me, are you?" I allow my meanness to take over completely.

"Geez, you're awful. No, I have a girlfriend that loves me and is way cooler than you. I never think about you. I would NEVER be interested in someone like you." *Ouch.* That one stung.

"I can get myself home," My voice is so high and fueled with rage that if it goes any higher, I will be screaming.

"I hope you get eaten by wolves or bears on your way." Dylan says this gem over his shoulder as he has already turned back to his house.

"*Really* nice, Dylan, you're such a gentleman."

"Whatever. Later, *May*." May echoes against the trees—bouncing around this wild land with such force that I bet every creature on this mountain can hear it.

As I stalk angrily towards my house, I wonder how we went from an awkward silence to fighting with each other in the matter of ten seconds. Not only did it happen abruptly, but it is also the first fight we have ever had and I cannot help but think about how much things have changed between us.

"Are you mad at me, Dyl?" I grip the rope tightly in my hands as I say this, fear circling my heart.

He tries to catch his breath, he is holding his knee between his hands, clearly in pain. Through gritted teeth he responds, "No, May. It's fine."

It's not fine and I know that. He trusted me with the rope and I let it go. I was not strong enough to keep it in my hands, the heat from the sun made my hands too slippery.

We spent this hot July afternoon at the creek, using a rope swung over a tree branch as entertainment. It is a simple game, one of us holds one end of the rope while the other uses it to swing back and forth over the shallow flow of water beneath. We have done this a million times before, but today, I dropped it. Dylan did a great job, allowing me to swing for at least ten minutes, but when I did it, he didn't even make it once before the rope slipped through my hands and Dylan landed on his knee on the stones below. It started bleeding immediately and I yelled his name.

I drop the rope and run over to where he is sitting on the side of the water's edge. He is rocking back and forth with his knee in his hands. I know he is in pain because his eyes are watering and Dylan never cries.

"Dylan, I'm so sorry. Can you walk? I can go get your mom if you can't." I am reaching for him now, wrapping my skinny arm around his chest.

"I'm okay, just give me a minute."

The once forgotten memory is now vivid.

He was not okay and twelve stitches and multiple lectures later, Dylan and I learned that while I was taller than him, that did not mean I was strong enough to hold a rope swing for him anymore. It was the first time in our friendship that I really even noticed that he was a boy and I was a girl and physically, that made us different. At only ten years old, it was not something I had ever really thought about before. Even though I failed and dropped the rope and he was hurt, Dylan never blamed me for what happened. He was never angry with me. In fact, I didn't even know if he was capable of anything other than slight annoyance. I never once saw him raise his voice or get mad and maybe that is why I am so startled by what just transpired between us.

The fact is that Dylan is *livid* with me. And I *hate* it.

Chapter Four

Dylan

She actually agreed to come to dinner.

After my mom argued with me for twenty minutes about inviting May, I hoped that she would just be her awful self and say no, but she didn't. What is her deal? One second, she acts like I am barely an acquaintance in the store, the next she wants to visit with my mom? This girl is too much.

For some stupid reason I am nervously trying to fix my hair and shave before she gets here. I know how pathetic it is that I care about what I look like in front of her, so this is not a proud moment for me.

The doorbell rings so I give up and shrug in front of the bathroom mirror. I know I'm not a bad looking guy. I've never had problems getting girls, and, in fact, am dating the one and only Candace who happens to be one of the hottest chicks on the planet and an extremely popular Instagram influencer, but there is just something about May that brings out all my insecurities.

It would not take a genius to say it probably has to do with the many nights I spent lying in bed wondering what I did wrong and how bad of a kisser I must be for her to never speak to me again.

I'm mortified to tell you that I was so stressed about what happened with May, that it took me until I was seventeen to even attempt to kiss someone again and, when I did, I had prepared and practiced on the back of my hand more times that I can count. After a few more girlfriends and some more practice with actual girls instead of my hand, I have since learned that I am not—in fact—the world's worst kisser.

The humiliation is only confounded by the year I sent

her handwritten letters that she never responded to. If there was a God, he would have made sure that each one of those letters got lost in the mail before May ever had the chance to read any of them. Or perhaps her mom threw them away before she ever saw them. I do not remember the exact words I wrote, but I do know that they were astoundingly pathetic.

Maybe it was all just a bad dream and I never actually did something that embarrassing. As I tell myself this, my reflection cringes. *Ugh.*

Taking a deep breath, I shake my arms hoping the embarrassment will roll off my skin and on to the floor. With another deep breath, I square my shoulders in an attempt to look as confident and unfazed as possible.

For a moment, while strutting downstairs, I actually believe that there is a chance that I could make it through this evening unscathed but the second I lay eyes on her— that confidence ghosts me harder than she did.

Whoa.

She always looks beautiful on her social media pages, but, right now, looking at her, it's impossible to act unaffected. The body that was hidden underneath oversized clothes at *The Corner Mart* is out of this world and my eyes are drawn to the way her jeans are hugging every inch. While I may have thought she looked the same she always has, I realize now that is not entirely true. Some things have certainly changed and the skinny girl who ran around this ranch is definitely a grown up. Blood rushes to the lower part of my body, annoying me with its response to her. My body seems to have forgotten how much she hurt me, but my heart sure hasn't.

We make eye contact and I know she caught me admiring her. Her blue eyes darken and I wonder if her pupils are as dilated as I know mine have to be.

Crap, I need to regain composure if I have any chance

of getting through this dinner with what little dignity I have left.

After one painful hour of forcing my eyes to look anywhere but at her, I'm now stuck walking her back to her house because my mother is apparently on a mission to make my life a living hell.

Maybe if I stare at the stars instead of her, I will be able to get through this but I can feel her eyes on me and it sends shivers down my back. She makes a sudden movement forcing me to acknowledge her.

"What?" I grunt at her, hoping my irritation is obvious.

"Nothin'." *Please* stop staring at me, I beg internally.

"Thanks for dinner." *Seriously?* She's thanking me?

"It was my mom's idea."

"Oh, yeah, I know. I just mean. . . well, thanks anyway."

"Whatever." I have zero desire to ease her obvious discomfort.

"Are you mad at me for something, Dylan?" She has *got* to be kidding.

"Are you kidding me?"

"No." This response is so irritating; I lose it *instantly.*

"You're one of the meanest, most self-absorbed people I know." A flash of regret hits me like a sledgehammer. *Keep it together, Dylan*, remember that you are supposed to be too cool to care.

"What? No, I'm not." Her eyebrows are high on her forehead, she has the audacity to act surprised by my insult which further fuels my irritation.

"Whatever, I see your social media pages, I see how

you are." I'm spiraling, this is not going to end well.

While May yells at me about how its normal to be on social media, or something along those lines, she gestures her hands wildly in the air. I definitely affected her. *Good.* I hope what I said settles under the top layer of her skin and burns like she burned me all those years ago.

"Is this all about when we were fourteen?" How *dare* she.

"No, I don't care about that anymore." Lies.

"You're not still obsessed with me, are you?"

Okay, I've had enough of this. Time to get the big guns out, "Geez, you're awful. No, I have a girlfriend that loves me and is way cooler than you. I never think about you. I would NEVER be interested in someone like you." Take *that*.

"I can get myself home." May's hands are on her hips now like that will somehow make her seem bigger than she really is. It is the first time I really notice just how little she is. I think she is the same height as she was when she was fourteen.

"I hope you get eaten by wolves or bears on your way." Okay, now I have gone completely over the edge.

"Really nice, Dylan, you're such a gentleman."

"Later, *May*." I say the nickname with a bitter bite of annoyance.

May scurries away with her arms crossed and her head down. Did I really just tell her that I hope she gets eaten by wolves or bears? If there was a hole I could crawl into and never come out of, I would.

To make this situation even more humiliating, I sit behind a tree and watch discreetly to make sure she gets home safely, like the true weirdo that I am.

"Yup, real cool, Dylan," I chastise myself out loud.

The moonlight is lighting her path and the sound of her footsteps are growing distant, but my heartbeat only gets louder as I keep replaying our exchange in my head.

Obviously, I am not as over what she did to me as I thought. Just a few days ago, I was excited for this summer but now my chest is filled with a sense of profound dread.

How am going to get through this with her here?

Chapter Five

Miranda

The door slams behind me, rattling the ceiling fan. My heart is beating against the walls of my chest as though it is trying to break free of the prison I have put it in.
Why?
Why is it that Dylan Ryder influences the rhythm of my beating heart? I get that he is angry with me but isn't this a bit of an overreaction? I mean, we were just kids. *Get over it already.*
The thoughts disturb every molecule in my body. *I would NEVER be interested in someone like you* rattles around in my head, bouncing off the layer of insecurity I shroud myself in.
I have spent so long carefully curating an image in my head of Dylan as being nothing other than just a boy I used to hang out with. While, *yes*, I had a brief crush on him the summer I was fourteen, and, *yes*, we kissed one time sitting atop our favorite boulder high above the sunflower field, that was it. We have never been in a relationship, we have never had sex, we have never had anything with each other outside of a childlike friendship and one brief moment when our lips touched. So how is it possible that after all this time my body is responding to him the way hummingbirds respond to a freshly bloomed flower—fluttering with restless energy?
While my heart beats with thoughts of Dylan, some darker emotions begin to trickle up from the depths. Anytime I think of him, it leads me back to this place and back to my parents' divorce, which inevitably leads me to memories I don't care to revisit. It is as though all the pain is connected somehow—each moment being responsible for the next. What most people do not

know—*correction*—what no one knows, is that when the small silver Toyota slammed into the large trunk of the tree that sits off Sycamore Road, it was not *really* an accident. I did not total my ex's car as the result of some reckless drunken decision to get behind the wheel, but instead it was an intentional act of self-destruction.

Desperate to quell the reality of what I did before it can fully engulf me, my feet lead me to the wine cellar. Taking two steps at a time in an uncoordinated and rushed attempt to reach the wine before my heart beats out of my chest, I trip, hitting the stone wall of the dank cellar with my forehead.

Crap, that is going to leave a mark.

Rubbing my palm across the stinging skin, I decide that I will deal with covering it up tomorrow, because all I can bring myself to care about right now is drowning out the feelings that are forcing their way to the top, threatening to burst through my skin.

This headache is undoubtably the worst headache I have ever had. You cannot convince me that anyone has ever had a worse headache than I do at this moment.

A single ray of morning light has made its way into my bedroom and is striking my eyelid which, in turn, is increasing the throbbing from a dull ache to full blown hammering.

I must move. I need to find Tylenol and drink water. If I do not, it is possible I will simply die from this.

I move with caution, not wanting the bomb in my head to explode. I slide my feet across the wood floor, slouching down as I do, the weight of the bomb apparently weighing me down.

This glass of water is not sufficient, so I lean my head on the inside of the freezer against a bag of frozen fruit—strawberries, I think. The crunchy icicles begin to soothe the flames in my skull.

The realization of what I have done begins to dawn on me. I got drunk—alone. *Again.*

I promised my parents that I did not have a drinking problem and that I would remain sober for the entire summer. Now, after binging twice, I will have to go into town to replace the two bottles of wine I stole from the cellar. I touch my finger to a sore spot on my forehead, reminding me of the fall.

Maybe I don't have as good of a handle on my drinking as I thought.

At the liquor store—the only one in town—aptly named *The Liquor Store*, I search out two bottles of wine that match the ones I took from the cellar and stand in line with my fake ID to purchase it. *Man, I hope this works.*

My phone rings as the cashier rings up the wine and does not even bother to look at my ID, "Hey, Mom."

"Morning, honey, what're you doing?"

"Just getting some stuff in town. What's up?"

"I need you to put in a small, fenced area."

"What? How the hell am I supposed to do that? And why would I do that?"

"The tenants need it for their little dog they are bringing. You don't need to do much; you just need to help Dylan with installing it. I don't want him to have to do it alone."

"Dylan? Are you kidding me?"

"No—I spoke to Betty last night to ask her if he would be willing, and she said sure. He is saving me money by doin' it as a favor. Look, Miranda, I know you have some weird hatred for the kid, but can you just be a grown up for once? I need this fence done."

"Fine." I roll my eyes so hard that my headache from this morning comes back in full force.

"He'll start working on it tomorrow around noon. Send me a picture when it's done."

"Fine."

Chapter Six

Dylan

I need space from her but can't seem to get it.

I mostly need space from those eyes and those hips. If I get too close, I may erupt into flames and be consumed completely. Of course, with my mom signing me up to build a friggin' fence for Lynn, I will have to interact with May for most of the day tomorrow.

May is dangerous territory for me. The truth is, I fell in love with her the moment I first saw her. Her family had just bought the house nearest our ranch and my mom brought me over so we could welcome them to the mountain. I was only six years old and bummed when she told me they had a girl my age instead of a boy. I thought girls were gross and silly at this point in my life. As I stood on the front porch holding the pie Mom made, the door swung open and when I saw long golden hair and a bright smile, I became hers instantly even though I didn't fully understand it until later.

Fast forward to when our lips touched on that hot July day, my heart melted into liquid gold and travelled from my chest through my body and onto May's lips. She took that piece of me with her—and she never gave it back.

The only way I was able to deal with the loss of her and that piece of me was by convincing myself that I was over her. I told myself that I never really loved her to begin with—mistaking youthful innocence for something real. Licking my wounds, I got through the rest of school just waiting for it to be over. All I ever cared about was getting back to this mountain. This place is where I'm happiest. Do not get me wrong, high school was not horrible. I had a few friends and a few laughs and did okay with a couple of girls, but overall, it was just a way to pass the time until I could get back here.

This ranch, this mountain, these trees, and the sunflowers is where I belong.

However, as I looked at her across the dinner table tonight, I knew I was still missing something. It's as though my heart still aches for the piece that I gave her, but the girl I gave it to, the girl who would laugh on a dime and thought the world was full of magic, is long gone.

In her place is Miranda and Miranda sucks.

I let out a frustrated growl, I don't want to think about this anymore but it's proving difficult. My mind is consumed with all things May. Relenting, I allow myself to indulge and drift further into my memory bank and grab one that was all but lost—until now.

"Do you think they're real?"

"May, you're crazy, there's no way fairies are real. We'd know by now."

"You're too close-minded, Dyl. You never see what I see. They have to be real. This world just makes more sense if they're real."

Never wanting to disappoint May, I relent, "Okay, you're probably right. You always are."

May turns her head to me, the sky blue of her eyes sparkling like water does when the sun hits it. She smiles wide and drops of sunlight surround her as she does, causing my skin to prickle and my blood to warm.

"You know you're my best friend right, Dyl?"

"Yeah. I know."

"Did you know that I think you're the coolest person on this planet?"

"Yeah. That's because I am." She laughs and I smile.

"What do you think of me?"

I think for a second, not yet sure how to put my

feelings into words, so I just say what comes to mind, "I think you're everything, May."

My body convulses in response to the memory. It's like it knows how unsafe it is for me to think of these things. My heart is still beating erratically as I lay in bed desperate for sleep to come.

To get May out of my head, I shift gears, giving myself a pep talk. "Things are great. I graduated high school, found *real* love with Candace, and am content. I don't need May." I say this out loud while simultaneously imagining Candace's perfect face and body. She is the type of girl guys only dream about, long legs and bleach blond hair, a face full of perfect makeup and lip filler to make her look almost Barbie-like. I am a lucky guy and I know it.

No matter how hard I try, though, the forced images of Candace are inexplicably shuffling between flashes of May.

Ughhhh, I have to shake this. I flip the pillow over and shove my face onto the cold side, stifling a frustrated scream.

Chapter Seven

Miranda

Dylan keeps repeating himself, huffing, and puffing as he unloads material from the back of his old Chevy, "My mom's makin' me do this. I didn't want to do this."

"I get it, Dylan. I don't want you here either, so can you make this quick?"

Dylan grabs a tape measure and begins to take measurements of the area for the fence. He also creates an outline in the grass of where the fence will go. He really seems like he knows what he is doing which I admit is causing me, and my body, a bit of unexpected heat.

"So, are you a fence expert or somethin'?" Wow, good one, Miranda.

"No, but I can do basic things, it's not that complicated . . . look, can you not just stand there staring at me?"

"Whatever, just don't screw it up." I stumble back into the house embarrassed for getting caught staring at him.

Once inside, I go to the sink to wash the dishes and try to ignore the view of Dylan out the window. This proves difficult because after an hour he starts sweating through his green t-shirt causing the fabric to cling to his body. I wish I could say that it was repulsive. I *really* do.

I don't know when Dylan got muscles but—*man*—did he get them. He is fit without being too bulky and looks like he has abs for miles under that tight t-shirt.

As the heat of day increases, I watch in awe as Dylan drops his tools and reaches behind him, pulling the sweaty fabric off and over his head in one swift motion. My mouth drops and my eyes go wide.

His back is—*whoa.*

His skin shimmers with sweat as he bends down to pick up the shovel again. I swear time slows to a near stop as I watch the movement. The rippling muscles with sweat cascading down their tight form might be the most erogenous thing I have ever seen. I didn't even know that I was into men's backs, but I certainly know now.

Then I notice something else—ink. He is too far for me to make it out but he definitely has a tattoo of something etched into his side, down his ribcage.

My head explodes into a bunch of tiny fires behind my eyes as my hormones take over. Suddenly overcome with shock at my reaction, I jolt back away from the window and drop a dish on the floor.

It is just a man's back, Miranda. *Get. It. Together.*

As I rub my dish-soapy hands through my hair and over my face in a desperate attempt to snap out of it, I hear him call my name. "Hey, Miranda? Come out here."

I practically race to the door—my hormones leading the way, "What is it?"

"There's somethin' buried here."

I walk over to him as he crouches down using his hands to dig something out of the dirt, while I try and fail to keep my eyes off his bare chest.

"What is it?" I repeat like a parrot.

"Dunno', but it's shiny so I know it's not a rock."

After a few minutes of digging, Dylan pulls out a small tin box. The tin is dented and dirty but still has some of its original silvery shine.

"Oh wow, what the heck is that?" For the sake of curiosity, I momentarily put aside my hatred—and lust for Dylan Ryder.

"Do you want to open it?" Dylan asks as he hands it to me. The sun hits his burnt sienna-colored eyes causing my knees go numb. Is it true? Is weak in the knees really a thing?

"Miranda?"

I jolt out of my head and remember that I'm meant to respond, "Sure. I hope it's money."

"I get some if it is." I almost laugh at this, but when I remind myself who it is that I am talking to, I stop myself.

The lid is stuck with time, making it difficult for me to open, but once I do, I let out a strangled gasp.

Oh no.

The sudden realization of what is in this unassuming tin slaps me across the face.

"What? What's in it?"

"Um, it's nothing. Look, Dylan, it's just garbage. I'll take it inside and throw it out. Can you get back to it? I don't want you here all day." God, I hope he drops it. The last thing I want is for him to know what is contained in this box.

"Why are you being so weird? Let me see it."

"No, it's nothing . . . and I'm not being weird, just drop it." I say this while simultaneously sprinting back inside the house.

"Whatever, May!" Dylan bellows behind me.

"It's Miranda!" I scream out in my wench-like howl.

The screen door slams behind me. My heart is racing, my palms are slick with sweat. Every emotion I have ever felt is swelling inside my chest at once. The overwhelming sensation causes me to reach for a remedy, any remedy. I race down to the cellar and take the first wine bottle I reach off the rack, grabbing the corkscrew that is strategically placed in my back pocket, and swig two big gulps down the second I get it open.

"What're you doing?" My heart stops, then shutters, then stops again.

I turn back to see Dylan standing on the steps of the cellar, bending slightly as confusion and concern etch across his features.

Panicked, I almost spit out the red courage, "Nothin', just taking a swig of this."

"Why?"

"No reason."

"Come on Ma—Miranda, what's the deal with the box? You're freaking out. What's going on?"

"It's just something I buried a long time ago, I completely forgot about it, and it startled me. It's nothing important, but you don't need to know about it." My overly loud voice and shaking hands are in stark contrast to the words spewing from my mouth.

"Okay, whatever, I don't care. I'll drop it."

"Good. Thanks."

Dylan pauses before saying, "Can you stop chugging wine now?"

My grip on the bottle is tight; my fingers are stiff with anxiety. The space around us feels smaller and the walls close in slightly. The nearness of Dylan's shirtless body to mine creates an awkwardness in both of us. He is turned slightly so I still can't make out the tattoo on his ribcage, though that doesn't stop me from trying. However, I *can* see the dark hair that stretches from his belly button to bellow the edge of his jeans.

"Miranda?! Did you hear me? Put the wine down." Apparently, the closeness of Dylan's bare chest has rendered me unable to speak.

"Oh, uh, yeah. I heard you. Bottle down." I set the bottle down and rip my eyes away from his beautiful body, forcing them to stare at the floor.

"Uh, okay, I'll get back to the fence . . . are you done being a weirdo?"

"Yes, of course. Just go away." His caring about me is making me uncomfortable in ways that are hard to put my finger on, so I spew bitterness at him. "Stop worrying about what I'm doin', Dylan, mind your own business."

"What's your problem, May? Why are you such a bitch to me? What did I ever do to you?" Dylan's face is reddening as he says this.

"I'm being a bitch to you?! You are the one who is so angry, Dylan, not me. I don't care at all. Not about this place or you!" I hate myself the second I spit the words out, knowing they are far from the truth, but my nerves are shot and I no longer seem to have control over what I say.

"Damn right I'm angry at you! You were awful to me and you just come here and expect me to forget all about it? You owe me an apology, May. I never deserved to be dropped like that without so much as a phone call. And you definitely have no right to be rude to me right now. I never did anything to you other than kiss you after you asked me to. Is that why you are acting this way?"

"No, Dylan. Let it go already. It was years ago—I don't care about that!" Please leave. *Now.* I beg internally as my heart begins to hurt from pounding so hard.

"Whatever. Just so you know, I don't care about that kiss or you either for that matter. So, get over yourself."

Dylan throws his hands in the air, briskly storming off, leaving me wounded in his wake.

I can't help but ask, *what is wrong with me?*

The small tin box was all but forgotten, residing in the deepest recesses of my mind.

The night I buried it had become unusually cold after the heat of the day was wiped away by a brief but powerful rainstorm. I sat at my window staring at the starless night while my dad packed up the vehicles so we could be on the road by dawn. My father was going to drive separate; this had never happened before. The changes to our dynamic had already begun. I did not know what my mother was doing, but I suspected she was in her bedroom alone and crying.

The house was eerily silent, even the ghosts kept still as the shock of what was happening washed over me. I remember crying. I remember crying more than I ever had in my entire life. It was as though my heart had been split open and its contents were pouring out of me in tear-shaped drops.

I was desperate for something to rid the pain so it occurred to me that I could bury it. I had watched Dylan's old sheepdog Billy bury sticks and bones all over the ranch. Dylan had told me it was a good way for him to save the items for a later date. I thought that maybe if I buried what I was feeling right now, I could avoid it until a later date. I thought that at a point when I was older, I would be wiser and much more capable of dealing with the pain. Feeling like I had a solid plan, I stepped away from my window and gathered up a few important items including a picture of my parents riding horses with me for my thirteenth birthday, the sunflower I drew when I was five that they framed and hung in the hallway, and, most embarrassingly, a letter to Dylan.

Presently, the box is sitting on the dresser across the room, moonlight bouncing off the dirty tin, creating a slight gleam. Apparently, that day of reckoning has come. An uneasy laugh escapes my throat. I'm no wiser nor more capable of dealing with this now than I was at fourteen.

Earlier after Dylan stormed off, I considered just throwing it away without looking inside, but could not bring myself to get rid of it. It is as though fragments of my soul are contained inside and if I discard them, then those parts of me would go with them.

With a deep breath, I peel off the covers and swing my legs off the bed. The floor is cold when it hits the soles of my bare feet. After dragging my reluctant body over to the dresser, I pick up the old box carefully, like it will explode if I move it around too much. It still has small clumps of dirt stuck to it, covering my fingertips with muddy residue as I lift the lid.

The first thing I see is the sunflower. It is drawn with a child's hand, the glass of the frame cracking slightly, mirroring my own broken heart. I had wanted to bury the drawing because I wanted to forget the sunflower field. It was no longer a magical or beautiful place to me—it was contaminated from the smoke emanating from the burning embers of my parents' marriage, staining the once bright petals.

I set the drawing aside, the feelings I had when I buried these items are still fresh. The next thing I see is the now yellowed photograph of my parents and me riding Dylan's horses. My birthday is in July and each year we would celebrate with the Ryders. I loved riding their horses, so each year it was the same: horseback riding during the day, cake and a bonfire at night. I had to let go of these birthday celebrations. I knew I would never be able to celebrate them the same way again. I remember my mother trying to convince me they could be the same if I just came back with her that next summer, but I knew in my heart that I could never come back here. It would never be the same without my dad. It was over.

I set the photograph down, right next to the sunflower drawing and pull out a folded piece of paper taped shut with a Lisa Frank unicorn sticker. I run my finger underneath the folded edge, tearing the sticker as I do. I open it up slowly, as if somehow that will make it easier to read.

Dylan- Today we kissed, and I loved it. But I must leave that kiss, you, and this place buried here in this box. I can't come back. It hurts too much. My parents have broken up and ruined our happy life. This house, these mountains, and you are stained with their betrayal. I will miss you, Dylan. I will miss your beautiful face and perfect lips. I will miss how funny you are. You are the best friend I have ever had. I love you so much and always will.
Forgive me,
May

Tears stream silently as I run my finger over the faded outline of lips and strawberry Chapstick. I vividly remember kissing the spot, transferring the kiss I had with Dylan to this piece of paper so that it too could be buried and forgotten.

In my fourteen-year-old mind, I thought I was solving a problem. I was unequipped to deal with the pain of what was happening, so I coped by shoving it aside to be dealt with at another date, burying these objects in the hopes that I could bury my pain with them. The startling realization that my coping strategies are no more efficient now than when I was fourteen hits me hard. How do I cope now?

Oh yeah, *I drink*.

Chapter Eight

Dylan

I was rough on her today. I realize that.

It's not without reason. After spending the night with her blue eyes haunting my dreams, I woke up in a panic. I do not want to blow my relationship with Candace, and I definitely do not want to go down the May path again. That road leads to nothing but heartache and rejection.

The sun is setting as I rock back and forth on the porch swing while Rusty sleeps by my feet. I mull over every word May said to me today and I am left as most men are most of the time: *confused*.

The tin box buried in the yard has me intrigued. Why did she not want to show me what was inside? Did it have something to do with me? Why was she chugging wine in the cellar? It was such an odd thing to do and something about it strikes me as unsettling. I have seen people chug beer, but *wine*? I also didn't fail to notice a bruise on her forehead that she did not have the last time I saw her. I would have asked her about it if I was not busy hating her so much.

My phone pings with a message from Candace, pulling me out of my contemplation.

Heyyy, call me later? Can't wait to see you!

It occurs to me as I type a message back that May has no idea that Candace and her parents will be her summer tenants. It also occurs to me that Candace has no idea that the person staying in the house with her, is in fact a girl that I was in love with for a large chunk of my life.

This already bad situation has the potential to become exponentially worse.

"What do you mean you were friends? Like when?"

"A long time ago when we were kids. I haven't spoken to her since I was fourteen. I had no idea she was going to be the one staying at the house this summer, I assumed it would be her mom."

"Is she someone I should be worried about?"

"No, it's nothing like that."

"Have you ever slept with her?"

"No, no. We were too young for anything like that."

"So, what did happen?"

"We just kissed, once."

"Oh, is that it? I don't care about that."

"Good, I just thought I should tell you."

"Awww, you're so sweet, Dylan."

"I am?"

"Yes . . . I can't wait to get there and see you. Where are we going to hook up? Your house?"

"Yeah, probably. It might be weird at Miranda's house since your parents will be there," and May, but I keep this thought to myself.

"Okay, it's been too long and I need to get naked, Dylan." What should be an exciting thing for a guy to hear from his girlfriend is laced with anxiety. *Oh no, I can't let May's presence here ruin my sex life.*

"Me too, I can't wait to see you."

"I have to get my beauty sleep. Call me in the morning?"

"Of course."

"And, Dylan, do me a favor and don't hang out with this Miranda chick."

"You don't have anything to worry about."

"Night."

"Night."

I think it best not to mention that I'm finishing up installing the fence at May's tomorrow. That is not 'hanging out' so *technically* I should be in the clear.

Chapter Nine

Miranda

After a restless night's sleep, filled with dreams of me calling out for Dylan over and over again and him turning his back to me each time, I wake with my clothes clinging to my body thanks to the layer of sweat beading on my skin.

Okay, *Okay*. Enough! I understand what the universe is trying to tell me.

I need to fix this.

If this year has taught me anything, it's that I need to grow up, so I will try to get him to forgive me and become friends again. Or at least, friend-*ly*. Hell, we only shared one kiss when we were fourteen. This should not be that big of an ordeal. I am no longer that girl who buried his memory in the yard, instead, I am a practical woman who is capable of being friends with a boy she used to be crazy over. As I tell myself this, I almost believe it. *Almost.*

My stress-filled sweaty dreams might continue until I redeem this relationship. The guilt from how I treated him is starting to pool inside my chest, forcing its way out through my pores, threatening to leak out into everything I do, tinting my life with its fury. Perhaps that is why the mere sight of him makes my skin burn.

He is right. I owe him an apology. But *how*?

It is ten a.m. and Dylan is already outside working on the fence, so I muster all my strength to go to him and make amends.

I push open the screen door and blurt, "Hey," wanting to sound casual but my voice squeaks.

"Oh. . . hey." We make eye contact for just a moment when he looks up causing my neck to heat.

"Can we be friends?" I force the words out as I hold my breath.

"What?" A crease has formed in his forehead.

"Do you think we can be friends again?" I stare at my feet as I say this.

"I didn't think you wanted to be my friend. You've been nothing but awful to me."

"I know. I'm sorry about that. I've just been going through some stuff, but I want to do better . . . So? Friends?"

"How're we supposed to be friends?"

"I dunno, it shouldn't be that hard, we used to be best friends."

"That was a long time ago, May, and you kind of destroyed our friendship."

"Come on, Dylan, quit holding a grudge."

He sighs and shrugs, "Sure, whatever, May."

"Great. Also, please call me Miranda. So, can I help you with this?"

"It would be helpful if you would just go back inside and let me get through this."

"Fine."

While he works, I congratulate myself on mending our relationship and decide to prove to him I mean it, so I find him on Instagram and send him a request to follow him. His account is private so I can't scroll through any pictures and figure out who his girlfriend is—not that I am interested.

I drop to the couch restless. For some reason, I still feel uneasy about Dylan. Why am I still feeling guilty?

Deep in thought, my phone pings, and I pick up to see that Dylan has accepted my Instagram request. Surely, this means he forgives me, *right*? Hopefully, I will be able to get some guilt-free sleep now.

I step back into the kitchen and peek out the window.

He has his phone in hand and is sitting under the shade of the pine tree closest to the house. A sudden flash back to Dylan sitting in that exact spot waiting for me to wake up to go with him on some adventure, lights up in my mind before I can stop it.

The morning sun is sprinkling in through the curtains in my room. I stretch my arms and lean towards them to push them aside to check for Dylan.

Right on schedule, he is waiting patiently under the pine tree that is slightly to the left of my bedroom window. He always sits there because he knows I can see him when I wake up.

A smile spreads across my face as I watch him resting with his forearms on his knees, his head leaning against the bark with the needles from the tree above casting shadows over his face. I don't know how long he has been there; I never know how long he waits for me, but he is always there—waiting.

To pull myself back from memory lane, I start scrolling through Dylan's Instagram and locate the girlfriend immediately. She is tall, blond, skinny, and totally hot.

Crap—I think she is even hotter than I am.

The images of them at concerts and on dinner dates are almost too much so I throw my phone down. The Dylan of today is far from the dorky childhood boy that used to play air guitar to make me laugh, and I don't know how to reconcile the two.

Suddenly, it dawns on me. Am I *jealous*?

Damn. I cannot go down this road. I cannot crush on him again, it's dangerous and stirs up all kinds of grief that I am not trying to awaken.

But how do I keep these feelings at bay?

"Okay, it's done." Dylan dips his head into the back door, clearly not wanting to come in farther than the threshold.

"The fence? Nice. Want lunch before you leave?"

Dylan scrunches his eyebrows together tightly, "Really?"

"Yeah, I told you we're friends now."

"Okay, Miranda. Lunch would be good." He says this with about as much enthusiasm as he would be for a root canal.

Dylan finally comes inside the house as I congratulate myself on really committing to this whole friend thing.

"So, are you ever going to tell me what's in the box?"

I sigh dramatically, "I thought you weren't goin' to ask me about that, remember?"

"Come on, just tell me. It must be good, or you wouldn't be so weird about it."

"Just drop it, please. It's more embarrassing than anything."

"Hmmm, I'll drop it. For now." A devilish smile spreads across his beautiful face and the air that was in my lungs suddenly escapes, leaving me gasping for more. It's the first smile he has gifted me with since I arrived back and I covet it—tucking it safely into a corner of my heart.

"My mom left some sammies at the house for me, we could go there and eat."

"Really? You're still saying 'sammies'?"

"What, was I supposed to get a new vocabulary once my voice dropped?"

"I guess I figured you were more of a grown-up now." I say this with a slight head tilt, hoping he sees that I'm trying to joke with him. Instead, he glares at me, so I forge ahead, changing the subject. "Okay, um, so you're inviting me to come with?" This comes out in such a labored manner; you would think I have never had a conversation with another human before.

"I guess."

"Gosh, you're sweet," I say sarcastically, hoping again to make him laugh. It does not.

"Just come on."

A couple of sandwiches and iced teas later, I convince myself that the awkwardness between us has begun to lift—although the silent chewing begs to differ.

"So, where's your mom?"

"She's in town. She might have some more of your mom's mail in Dad's office, let's check before you go."

Dylan's dad died when he was only three years old, so he has no memory of him, yet he still calls the office his dad's office. His mother never remarried, and she also still talks about him like he is alive. I always thought it would make it more painful for Dylan to talk about him like he was still here, but he has never said anything about it so maybe it's comforting for him.

Dylan rummages around the office while I sit in the leather chair in front of the grand desk that is still crystal clear in my memory. It is an intricately detailed large piece of oak with scratches on the right side from where Dylan and I smashed into it while playing pirates when we were just seven years old.

"Remember when we made these scratches?" I ask this without thinking, running my fingers along the grooves.

Dylan glances my direction but goes back to what he is doing, "Not really."

"I do. We really have a lot of memories together.

Whenever I think of my childhood, I think of you." *Why am I saying these things?* Did I hit my head on the cellar wall harder than I thought?

Dylan drops his arms, "I don't know what to say to that, Miranda."

"Do you think of me when you think of your childhood?" Okay, I have completely lost all control of what is coming out of my mouth now.

Dylan shrugs in response, further driving the nail into my coffin so I drop it. Maybe the awkwardness is not lifting as much as I hoped—or at all.

"Did you find anything?"

"Yeah, here's a letter that looks like it's just junk mail." Dylan hands me the thin envelope. As he does, I notice a small tattoo on his wrist for the first time. Hmm, another tattoo? I find this more interesting than I probably should.

"Hey, what's that?"

"What?"

"Is that a tattoo?"

"Oh, yeah. It's just a heart."

"Oh, it looks kinda wobbly."

"It is. My grandma drew it before she died."

"What? Grandma Beth died?"

"She died about a year ago."

"Oh. I'm sorry, I didn't know."

"Of course you didn't, why would you?" My mouth drops as I can see the anger is back and etched across Dylan's face.

"You're so angry with me, Dylan, is there no way we can be friends again?" I say this quietly while feeling my face flush.

Dylan is shaking his head as he responds, "I don't see it happening. Our friendship died a long time ago when we were kids. You know, you haven't actually apologized to me. Saying we should be friends and sending me an Instagram request is not an apology. Look, I have to go, can you let yourself out?" The sharp tone he uses and clenching in his jaw conveys just how serious he is.

"Oh—okay." I turn quickly and leave before he can see the tears in my eyes.

Why am I so upset about Dylan? Did I really think I could blow him off for so long and he would not care? I think about the summer after we kissed and how I told my mom I would stay with Dad during the summers from then on. I remember how shocked she was.

"Why wouldn't you want to come to the mountain for the summer? You can help me figure out what to do with the property. I'm thinking we could rent the place out for the summers. It could be fun. Besides, you have gone every summer for years, it wouldn't be right if you stopped now. You love that place. Dylan is going to be so upset that he doesn't have his friend."

"I don't care about Dylan, Mom. I have a life here; I don't want to leave my friends—my actual friends, so I'll just stay with Dad."

"What do you want me to say to Dylan? You know he'll ask about you. He's been calling and sending letters for months, May, can't you just call him and talk to him?"

"No, Mom, just drop it. Tell him I've died or something. It doesn't matter."

"Wow, May, this attitude of yours is rough."

"Whatever. And I told you to call me Miranda from

now on."

I cringe as I think about how bratty I was to her and how Dylan must have felt when I did not show up that summer, or ever again. What did he think? He must have assumed he did something wrong. Hopefully, I didn't scar him too much. Of course, he has a hot girlfriend now, so it seems like he is doing just fine.

My chest aches and I recognize it as guilt. Obviously, my lame attempt at mending our friendship was not sufficient.

I press a hand to my chest as I think about all the letters he wrote and how I refused to open them and for the first time since I was fourteen, I wonder what he wrote in them.

What would a mature person do in this situation? That is what my mom is always asking me now. I guess a mature person would apologize to Dylan.

A *real* apology.

He deserves it for what I did to him and maybe it will finally put my guilt to rest and stop him from being so angry with me.

Now, how do I do that? Should I write him a letter?

The thought is so absurd that I laugh out loud but I still grab a piece of paper and begin to write. I am too nervous to apologize in person, so I guess this will have to do.

> *Dylan- I just wanted to tell you that I'm sorry. I'm sorry for ghosting you after that summer and after we kissed. I'm sorry that I blew up our friendship and refused to come here again. I can understand why you are mad at me. I want you to know that it wasn't you. That day, after we kissed, my parents told me*

they were getting divorced. I became so depressed that I convinced myself that love was just an illusion to be avoided at all costs. I took out my depression and anger on this place, and on you. I don't expect you to forgive me, but I wish you would. I have missed our friendship and I feel like a real ass.
Think about it, please. – Miranda

Now to get the note to him. I do not want to put it in the Ryder mailbox or just go over there and knock on the front door because I definitely do not want Mrs. Ryder to know anything about this.

Ah ha! I can sneak it to him by climbing on the roof and slipping it onto the desk that sits underneath his window just as I did when we were kids. It is still early enough that he should not be asleep yet but is probably downstairs watching TV with his mom.

Throwing my shoes on, I race out of the house, note—and brilliant idea—in hand.

Okay, so maybe not so brilliant of an idea after all.

This thought occurs to me as I clutch a tree branch for dear life, realizing just how idiotic I truly am.

The breeze is so intense that I barely make it when I leap onto the roof from the old pine tree closest to their house. The loud thud that occurs when I crash down is a lot louder than it did when I was a kid, but of course that was thirty pounds ago. How did I used to do this all the time?

I'm on all fours inching my way over to Dylan's window. The idea that sneaking up to someone's window after dark is not only stupid but could lead to a lot of awkwardness suddenly dawns on me. What if he is naked or something?

Oh man, this is such a bad idea, but it is too late to turn back now.

I take a deep breath and convince myself to be brave while silently easing myself into a sitting position. I gently push up the window one inch at a time, careful to be as quiet as a mouse. The room is dark and the curtains are drawn, so I cannot see inside yet.

Suddenly, the end of a large object comes through the curtains, barely missing my face thanks to my quick reflex to throw my head back.

"WAIT, don't! It's me, Dylan!" I bellow out into the wind hoping to thwart the attack.

Dylan rips back the curtains, "What the hell!? You scared me. I thought you were a coon or somethin'!"

"Sorry, I'm so sorry." I *cannot* believe this is happening to me.

"What're you doing here!?"

Dylan is only in his boxers, the moonlight is illuminating his muscular body, highlighting the way his chest is rising in an increased tempo. I'm rendered speechless by the sight of him shirtless, yet *again*.

"Miranda?! I said what're you doin' here?"

"I'm sorry, I'm an idiot. I wrote you a note and wanted to get it to you, but I didn't want your mom to see it, so I thought I'd sneak it onto your desk like we did as kids. It was dumb." The words are tumbling out of my mouth at a furious pace.

"Dumb is an understatement, May." In light of how ridiculous I am being, I decide not to correct him on the nickname. That feels pretty minor at this moment.

"Here," I say, handing him the now crumpled piece of paper.

"Look, I'm too old for this kind of thing," he says while refusing to take the paper from my hand, "can you just say what you want?"

"Um, well, sure. I guess. It's just embarrassing."

Dylan holds his gaze, making me feel small . . . and stupid.

"Okay, I'll read it." I open the note and read it quickly, the words quiet and rushed, my hands shaking with embarrassment.

Dylan remains silent, torturing me.

"Well? Do you forgive me or not? If you don't, then screw you." I'm audibly louder now.

"Wow, you're terrible at apologies."

"Ugh, whatever," I say as I turn to get off the roof.

"Hold on, hold on. Can you come in? You don't need to crawl on the roof like a lunatic."

I roll my eyes and slide inside Dylan's bedroom, "Where's the desk that used to be here?"

"I moved it out years ago. Did you think my room would look the same as it did when we were kids?"

"Oh, no, I guess not."

"Look, Miranda, I don't want to hold a grudge. I've been pissed at you for the longest time, but it seems stupid now. I'm over it. I forgive you and, yes, we can be friends again. Or at least friend-*ly*."

"Thanks for forgiving me. I really am sorry about how I treated you."

Dylan is sitting on the edge of his bed now; the curtains are flowing in the breeze causing the shadows in the room to dance. He runs his hand through his inky black hair, making me wish I could run my hands through it, too.

He takes a deep breath. "I was devastated. I was crazy over you, and you were my best friend. You never spoke to me, never told me why. I spent years thinking that I must've done something wrong." Unexpected tears have filled my eyes now, threatening to overflow. I haven't cried in front of another person since I was thirteen and fell and broke my arm when Dylan and I were climbing trees.

"You never did a single thing wrong. I was just so devastated about my parents. I didn't know what to do, so I pushed you away. It was like this place, and you, just reminded me of my parents. I messed up," I wipe my cheek, the tears flowing freely now.

"Hey, please don't cry, Miranda. It's okay, I forgive you. We're friends. It's water under the bridge." Dylan stands up as he says this, coming over and wrapping his arms around me.

The feel of my head laying on his chest and the warmth of his skin on mine is electric. My body awakens and shivers. Dylan must feel it too because he lets go and abruptly steps back, a look of regret carved across his face.

"You'd better get home."

"Yeah, definitely."

"Are you okay to walk yourself?"

"Oh yeah, I'm fine."

"Here, take this bat with you and text me when you get back."

"I don't have your number."

"Give me your phone and I'll put it in."

I hand Dylan my phone and watch him as he puts his number in as the moonlight shimmers across his face.

I exit quickly and quietly and spend the walk home trying desperately not to think about Dylan's chest or the way I felt in his arms.

I text "here" as soon as I am back in the house, Dylan responding with a thumb's up emoji.

I lay in bed and stare at that emoji for at least thirty

minutes before falling into a night of restless sleep with forbidden dreams.

Chapter Ten

Dylan

Thud.
What was that?
Thud.
Sounds like it is on the roof. Must be a racoon or something. Sounded kind of heavy to be a racoon, though. I better grab my bat.
I can hear shuffling, then a sound at my window.
What the hell?!
I swing my bat to try to hit the animal before it gets into my bedroom.
"Wait, don't! It's me, Dylan!"
"What the hell!? You scared me. I thought you were a coon or somethin'!"
"Sorry, I'm sorry." Oh my god, why is she here—outside my bedroom window of all places? Her eyes are wide as she looks me up and down and I suddenly feel very exposed as I stand here in just my boxers.
"Miranda?! I said what're you doin' here?"
"I'm sorry, I'm an idiot. I wrote you a note and wanted to get it to you, but I didn't want your mom to see it, so I thought I'd sneak it onto your desk like we did as kids. It was dumb."
"Dumb is an understatement, Miranda."
"Here."
"Look, I'm too old for this kind of thing. Can you just say what you want?" I really need her to leave.
"Um, well, sure. I guess. It's just embarrassing . . . Okay, I'll read." May reads the note quickly, the words stumbling out awkwardly. She is clearly nervous. The note is an attempt at an apology and while I want to stay mad at her, it is getting harder and harder to hold onto

this grudge.

Apparently, I do not respond to her apology quickly enough because she jumps down my throat, "Well? Do you forgive me or not? If you don't, then screw you."

"Wow, you're terrible at apologies, but hold on, hold on. Can you come in? You don't need to crawl on the roof like a lunatic."

I watch as May slides in through my window just like she did when we were kids and I try not to stare at her midriff when her shirt catches on the windowpane, pulling it up over her bellybutton. She struggles a bit to get inside, her feet dangling above the floor. I should help her, but my sudden awareness of her closeness to me, in my bedroom, with me in my underwear, is not a good situation and I need to get her out of here before I really embarrass myself with my betraying body.

"Look, Miranda, I don't want to hold a grudge. I have been pissed at you for the longest time, but it seems stupid now. I'm over it. I forgive you and yes, we can be friends again. Or at least friend-*ly*." I will say *anything* to get her out of my room right now.

"Thanks for forgiving me. I really am sorry about how I treated you."

I sit down on the bed, hoping the shadows will hide my growing attraction to her and while I am desperate to get her out of my space—I also want answers, so here goes nothing, "I was devastated. I was crazy over you, and you were my best friend. You never spoke to me, never told me why. I spent years thinking that I must've done something wrong." The weight of what happened between us is heavy as it drops from my lips before I have a chance to think.

May's eyes go wide before she responds, "You never did a single thing wrong. I was just so devastated about my parents. I didn't know what to do, so I pushed you away. It was like this place—and you, just reminded me of my parents. I messed up."

Tears stream silently from her eyes now, which is not what I was not expecting. I have only ever seen May cry once and so I have no idea how to handle this moment. Desperate to stop the flow of water leaking from her face, I go in for a hug, which—given the growing circumstances—is not my brightest move, so I let go of her swiftly.

May is the only person I have ever met that manages to look beautiful while crying. I shake the thought out of my head quickly as I watch her pull the door shut behind her.

After she leaves, I use every ounce of strength I have not to think about her. An uncomfortable thirty minutes later I finally fall into an edgy night's sleep.

Frustratingly, the blue from May's eyes and the moonlight dancing along her mid-drift make their way into my dreams, relentlessly tormenting me, transporting me back in time.

Knock. Knock, knock.

I know it's May. She is the only person in the entire world who knocks on my window late at night.

I tiptoe over and push the window up, allowing her to slide inside. She sits on the edge of my desk before jumping off. May is little, at fourteen years old, she appears to have stopped growing any taller and her short stature has always made it difficult for her to get in through the window without the help of my desk, so I leave it there for her to make her 'breaking in' easier.

This is the first year that I am taller than her and it is suddenly by a lot, at least three inches. I have to say that I love it. I know it's silly to be excited about being taller than a girl but it's a big deal to me. I like feeling like I can properly take care of her now.

Ever since we were about ten years old, May has been sneaking into my room late at night. She climbs the tree and jumps onto the roof with ease. We have always done the same thing when she sneaks over: created a fort under the blankets and used a flashlight to read adventure books and to discuss plans for our own adventures. Or just talk. May loves to talk and I love to listen to her. She likes all things magic and fairies and mysteries. I could listen to her for hours.

I have noticed that this year whenever she sneaks over, though, it feels . . . different. I now know that I am completely in love with her and my hormonal body likes to remind me of it. I think that is why these visits feel different to me. May doesn't seem to notice, though, so I try to hide it as best I can.

We curl under the blankets on my bed and I turn the flashlight on. It lights up our legs that are touching at the knees.

Instead of diving into a book or discussing where fairies might live on the ranch, May stays quiet. She is rarely quiet, so I know something is wrong immediately.

"Everything okay?"

"Hmm . . ." She leans back on my pillow, and traces the dinosaur print as she does. I internally chastise myself for still having such kid-like sheets. "I don't know. My parents are being weird."

"How so?" I lean back with her, propping the blanket up on the bright end of the flashlight to keep it from touching our faces while she talks.

"I dunno. It was odd. They didn't speak at dinner at all. I think they're fighting or something. I don't know why. They seemed fine yesterday."

"I think it's normal for parents to fight, May. It's probably not a big deal."

She scrunches her face in contemplation before responding, "Yeah, maybe. But you know how they are, they never fight. At least I don't think they do. They seem so happy all the time, I just don't know what is wrong with them today."

This reminds me of something from earlier that I had all but forgotten about. "Must be something in the water then because my mom has been super weird today, too. After we got back from the sunflower field, she was laying on her bed crying. She didn't even make dinner. I had to eat a frozen pizza."

"Really? Mrs. Ryder never cries. What the heck is going on, Dylan?"

I shrug and pick at a loose string hanging off the blanket draped over us, "They'll get over it. Don't worry about it, May."

May shakes her head and moves on, diving into a story about some lights she saw on the walk over here and how they have to be some kind of mystical presence.

I listen with interest as I watch her mouth form words and her eyes go wide with details. Gosh, she's beautiful.

I bolt upright out of bed in a thick sweat. The memories that have been flooding back ever since May returned have to stop. I'm not sure how much more of these I can handle.

The door creaks open. I'm in too deep of a sleep to bother opening my eyes to see what is going on, but I manage to mumble "Mom, is that you?" into my pillow.

"Dylan? Sweetie? You need to get up."

"Uh, what for?"

"It's five a.m. you need to get up, Sally's missing." *This* catches my attention.

I bolt upright, "Are you sure?"

"She's not in the stable. I can't find her anywhere. She must've escaped last night. I might have forgotten to shut the barn door and you know how ornery she can be." Mom is looking at me with wide eyes, but something seems off. I would expect her to be freaking out more than she is.

Sally only escaped one other time when I left the barn door open when I was eight or nine years old. May and I had been playing hide and seek and when I found May hiding in Sally's stall, I chased her out of the barn all the way back to the house. We laughed the entire time. We did not know what we had done until my mother went to feed the horses dinner and saw that Sally was gone. I was so worried that we had lost her forever, I cried the entire time we looked for her. It's one of the few times I have ever cried. Luckily, we found her within a couple of hours and after my mother lectured me for days, I never forgot to shut that door again. In fact, she still checks with me to make sure I remembered to shut it. So, I am understandably completely confounded right now that my mother would made this mistake.

"You forgot to shut the barn door? That's so unlike you."

"I know, I know. Don't give me too hard of a time. I also forgot to fix the hatch on her stable door so she gets out of the stable sometimes, but if the barn door is shut, I know she is safe and can't go anywhere. Guess I just forgot." She shrugs innocently, but I'm not buying it.

"Is there something you're not telling me?" I am standing now, searching for something to wear.

"No, I know it's not like me, Dylan, but I was really tired last night, and I made a mistake. Please just find her."

"Okay. It's okay, Mom. I'll get my shoes on and go find her."

"Listen, Dylan, I can't go with you. I have to take care of the ranch today, but I don't think it would be wise if you go alone. I want you to take May with you."

"What? No way. I can do it alone."

"There's supposed to be a storm later. It's not safe to go alone, you know you don't get cell service if you have to go high up to find her."

"What help is May in that situation?"

"I won't worry as much if you aren't alone."

"Mom, I really don't want to take May with me."

"Dylan—I'm not asking. Be sure to pack a bag with the essentials."

The sun is still sleeping.

The moon is still visible, and the birds have not yet started chirping.

The *last* thing I should be doing right now is trekking along the path to May's house to wake her up. She is going to think I'm completely crazy and after last night's bizarre window visit, I'm not too eager to be around her.

The cool morning air forces me to pull the hood of my sweatshirt up over my head. I hate it when my ears get cold. I rub my hands together as I try to figure out how I'm going to do this. I tried to text her, but she did not respond, so I guess I will have to pound on the front door until she wakes up.

I rehearse a few ideas as her house closes in, "Sorry to wake you, Miranda, my mom wanted me to see if you would come with me to help me find Sally. She escaped."

No, that's not it. "Sally escaped and my mom wants you to come with me to find her. Sally escaped and I need your help." Ugh, I'm going to sound like an idiot. I rub my hands over my face in frustration.

I have one foot on her porch when the front door flies open, "Sally escaped?" May is dressed in long pink pajama pants that are way too big on her and a large shirt with a sunflower printed on it. This—I notice immediately.

"Uh, yeah."

"Your mom called. Let me get dressed and I'll be right out."

"'Kay." I can't help but notice how cute she is with her hair frayed wildly around her face, then I chastise myself for noticing.

This is going to be a long day.

Chapter Eleven

Miranda

This is going to be a long day.

Even with this knowledge, I still have to help search for Sally. She was my favorite horse when I was a kid. She was who I wanted to ride each year for my birthday. Plus, I do not really have an excuse since Mrs. Ryder called me and pleaded with me to help. I would never want to disappoint her.

I throw on my best fitting jeans and a t-shirt and pull my hair quickly into a bun. I frantically brush my teeth and squeeze my cheeks to give myself some natural blush before running out to meet Dylan. I debate about putting on some makeup, but I fear he would notice and think I was doing it to impress him.

I step outside and Dylan looks up. We make brief eye contact, and my heart betrays me by practically leaping out of my throat. I manage to hold it in place by swallowing it back down, desperately hoping Dylan fails to notice my momentary reaction to the sight of him.

He turns abruptly, "Let's start on the north trail. Sally goes on that trail a lot when we ride her, so I'm hoping that's where she headed."

"Okay . . . I hope we find her. Does she do this a lot?"

"Only that one other time when we were kids."

"Yeah, I remember that."

We begin hiking up the north trail as I follow Dylan in silence. The sun is waking up, its light just beginning to soften the edges of the night.

It's been *three* hours.

Three long, desperately quiet hours.

"I just don't understand. This is her favorite trail. I don't even think I've seen a fresh hoofprint out here. I think we might need to try the west trail." These are the first words uttered from Dylan since this terrible morning began.

"Can I have some of your water?" My throat scratches when I speak.

Dylan nods as he pulls off his backpack and grabs me some water. "Do you need a break?"

I do, but I want to seem more in shape than I really am, so I lie, "No, I'm good. Just thirsty."

"This might take all day, Miranda, so if you ever need a break, tell me." *Oh. My. Gosh.* All day alone with Dylan? My heart might explode from awkwardness by noon.

"Oh, okay. No problem."

"Come on, let's cross over to the west trail. We go on that one sometimes so maybe we can find her around there."

It is only just after eight in the morning, but the weather is already getting weird. When you get this high up in the mountains, it can be hot one second, raining the next, then hot again.

Two more hours later and the weather is not the only thing that has been weird. I'm beginning to think that Dylan has completely forgotten that I am here. This is the most I have ever been ignored in my entire life.

"My mom packed a small lunch, so if we don't find Sally we'll stop about noon, okay?" He speaks!

"Okay." *Man*, I wish this would end.

Chapter Twelve

Dylan

It is so hard to focus on finding Sally when all I can think about is how May is right behind me. Should I talk to her? What do we even have to talk about? It might be best to keep ignoring her and walk in silence, but the tension is almost unbearable. On more occasions than I care to admit, I glance behind me as subtly as possible. May's head is down, and I notice her hair is sticking to the side of her face. She must be struggling and needs to rest, but she never says anything which does not surprise me. That is one thing that has not changed, she has always been overly competitive and proud.

"No, Dyl. I'm fine."
"May, you're bleeding."
"It's just a scrape. Let's keep going."
The boulder—our favorite boulder—is massive and May took a tumble trying to slide down. Her shin is red with dirt stuck to the skin that's peeled back. I know she wants to cry but refuses. She is always so concerned about being tough.
"Come on, May, it's me. You don't have to be tough in front of me." I say this hoping she will let me convince her to go home.
The blue of her eyes brightens, "I know. You're my best friend in the whole world, Dylan."
I smile. "I know."

This memory escapes me as sadness fills the space it leaves behind. The trust we had for each other is long gone now. In its place is nothing but pain.

"It's about noon and I'm starving. Cool with you if we

sit to eat for a minute?"

May looks up in relief, "Sure, if that's what you want. Or we can keep going." I can tell she does not really mean that though as she has already stopped walking.

"You wanna eat on the boulder?"

"*The* boulder?" May's face contorts as she says this.

"Yeah, it's just over there. It's better than sitting on the ground." I instantly regret suggesting the boulder. It means more to us than just a place to sit and eat lunch and I must have had a stroke that rendered me momentarily an idiot to suggest it.

"Oh, okay. I didn't remember it being so far away when we were kids."

"That's because we didn't use the trails but would cut right through. We can check for Sally in the sunflower field while we are there."

I make my way over the small creek that separates this trail from the sunflowers. They are just over a hill now. I have not been back to see them since May's fifteenth birthday, the first summer she did not come back. I shake my head abruptly, that is another memory I do not want to think about right now. Especially with her here.

It has been so long that it occurs to me that I do not even know if the sunflowers are even there anymore.

My feet get wet as the water in the creek is deeper than I expect, I look behind me to make sure May makes it over okay. She is close behind me now as I follow the overgrown path that leads to the field. My heartbeat quickens as more memories come flooding back. I push back some thick brush and the sun hits my eye. The yellow of the sunflowers practically glow in this light.

"*Sunflowers.*"
"*I figured.*"
"Of course, they're my favorite flower. How could

they not be?"

"What do you like about them?"

"I like that they're really tall. I really like the yellow of their petals. It's so pretty. Especially against the blue mountains and blue sky."

"Girls and flowers. So weird."

"You're such a boy. You don't like the sunflowers?"

The truth is that, no, I don't care at all about sunflowers. What I like about being here is that I'm here with her. I like the way her face lights up the second she lays eyes on them every time we come here. It's fascinating to me that she could be excited for something she has seen a million times. I also like the way her eyes match the color of the sky on a warm day, but I keep these thoughts to myself. If she knew what went on in my head, she would never speak to me again. Plus, I'm pretty sure she does not think of me as anything more than a friend.

I have always loved May, but this summer has changed everything; I have seen her in a new light. My innocent love for her is not so innocent now. She has pretty eyes and full lips and it's all my fourteen-year-old brain can think about. But I can't risk anything because May is not just any girl, she is THE girl and the last thing I want to do is for our friendship to end.

"So. Dyl. Have you kissed anybody yet?"

"No." I say this as casually as I can, hoping to conceal my shock at her very unexpected question.

"Me neither. I was thinking, maybe we should just kiss each other and get it over with. I'm tired of being the only girl in my class that hasn't kissed a boy yet."

"Uh . . . sure." This response is all I manage to muster as my throat has tightened significantly. She wants to kiss me? My hands are instantly sweaty as I stare at the bald eagle overhead. If I look at her, she will

be able to see how nervous I am, it's written all over my face.

"How 'bout tomorrow? At noon? At our spot?" Has she given this some thought?

"Okay." This comes out way squeakier than I intend. Darn changing voice.

I can see May smile out of the corner of my eye and I absently wonder if it's possible to die of happiness. Does she feel the same way for me as I do her?

"WOW." May's voice jolts me back to the present.

"Oh . . . yeah." This is all I can manage as the beauty of the sunflower field unfolds before us. There are hundreds of them. The blue of the mountains is a stunning contrast to the vast shimmering yellow. "I forgot how cool this was." The sentiment escapes my lips before I think of something better to say.

"Really? You don't come here all the time?" May's eyes are as big as mine as she takes in the view.

"Oh—uh—no. I haven't been here in some time." I'm intentionally vague, I don't want her to know that without her, I can't seem to bring myself to come here.

"How could you resist? If I was here as much as you, I'd make may way to the sunflowers at least once a week."

The wind blows slightly, wafting the slight nutty aroma all around us. It's a scent that I recognize immediately.

"I dunno. Just have other things going on at the ranch when I'm here." I shrug to sound nonchalant, hoping May drops the subject. It works as she stops talking, instead taking the lead towards the boulder. The sun radiates off her hair as she does, transporting me back in time again. This time to when we were even younger.

"There's a ladybug on you."

"Where?" May lifts her head slightly off the ground. I point to the small red bug moving slowly along the bare skin of her forearm. Before she can panic—she does not like insects crawling on her skin—I jump to save her.

"I'll get it." I pick up the bug, careful not to squish it, and place in on the stem of the sunflower next to May's shoulder.

"It's gone."

May turns her head towards me, her hair in swirls all around her, creating a shimmering halo, "Thanks. You're the best." She smiles wide and my heart skips in my chest. It's an unusual occurrence that only seems to happen when May is around. I should probably have it checked out.

"Don't you forget it."

May's smile widens more, "I won't."

But she does. She does forget.

Chapter Thirteen

Miranda

Maybe sunflowers have magical powers.
Yeah, that sounds reasonable.
Maybe sunflowers will fill Dylan with fond memories of us and he will suddenly forget what I did to him when we were fourteen. He will think about how close we once were, and we will pick up right where we left off as though nothing bad ever happened.

These are just some of the crazy thoughts I have while trudging through the tall stems of the sunflower forest. I know he said last night that he forgives me when I crawled all over his roof like a true maniac, but I need him to *really* forgive me and after spending the entire morning walking in silence, I can see that we are not even close to that.

Leaves tickle my arms and shoulders. The sensation is so familiar that it immediately teleports me to when I was a child.

We made it. They are surrounding us now.
The sunflowers.
I don't know if I can really put into words why I love the sunflowers as much as I do. It's hard to describe. It is more about the way they make me feel. The second I see one, my entire body warms while the thoughts of the day fade away. I'm instantly at peace.

They are more than just a beautiful flower, they are magical. They have to contain magic because that is the only possible explanation for how they could affect me so much.

I am ahead of him by a few feet now, the sweat on the

back of my neck drips down onto the rim of my t-shirt. Man, I really hope he does not see how sweaty I am. He, of course, appears completely unbothered by this long hike. His fit body only adds to my insecurity right now. To make matters worse, the light red shade on my forearms indicates that I probably should have thought to put on some sunblock. By the time we find Sally, I will look like a roasted tomato.

As if he can hear my thoughts, Dylan says, "You're getting sun-burned."

"Am I?" I say this as if I did not already know. "Shoot . . . You know what I remember the most about this place?" I work quickly to change the topic.

"What's that?"

"The smell."

"The smell? Really?"

"Yeah, did you know smell is tied more to memory than any other sense?"

"Hm, what does this place smell like then?"

"To me, it's a fresh smell. The smell of the wind, the pine, the grass. It's fresh and airy. You know?"

"Yeah, I guess I do. The sunflowers have a specific smell."

"Yeah, you're right. It's an unusual scent that I don't think I have ever come across anywhere else. Nutty, or earthy. Or both." Dylan nods, giving me all the encouragement that I need to keep talking. "What about you? What do you remember most about this place?"

"Um, I dunno." Dylan runs his hand through his hair as though he is frustrated. I carry on.

"It doesn't have to be just here with the sunflowers. What about being on the mountain? Or at your ranch? What is your favorite thing about it here?"

Dylan takes a long moment before responding. I keep foraging ahead toward our boulder, but I can hear him contemplating behind me.

"Probably the night sky. The stars are so bright here. Sometimes I go up on my rooftop to look through my telescope. It's incredible. I miss it during the winter when I'm back in Boulder."

"Oh man, I would love to do that," I say this without thinking and turn back to see Dylan's confused face. His eyebrows are scrunched together, and I realize that sitting on the rooftop looking at the stars is something that a girlfriend does, not a former childhood friend that you cannot stand to be around, so I correct myself.

"Maybe I can borrow your telescope one night." I say while congratulating myself on the quick save.

"Sure, Miranda."

An eagle soars overhead, taking this place to an almost majestic level. I cannot believe I have not come here every chance I could over the years. Being here now, it's hard to believe I ever stopped.

"There are dark clouds rolling in from the west, we might get caught in it."

"Oh, I didn't even notice them."

"They're coming in fast."

"How long do we have?"

"Eh, at least an hour."

Dylan and I reach the other end of the field and stand in front of the boulder.

The boulder.

We both turn around without thinking, doing as we always did and admire the view before sliding up backwards onto the rock.

Perched up on the rock with our feet dangling over the edge, the sunflower field stretches before us. The large flowers are dotting the landscape with their bright yellow hue. Storm clouds hover over in the distance, muting part of the field's brightness. The mountains grow dark thanks to a shadow cast by the incoming clouds—deepening their sky-blue shade into a deep ocean blue. The untouched land is on full display before us, in all its glory.

Sitting to Dylan's right, I instinctually run my fingers over the engraving between us. Our initials and a *'was here'* etched below them.

It's Tuesday. I know that because my parents have their weekly date night on Tuesdays, and they left a couple of hours ago to head down the mountain. On Tuesday night date nights, my parents let me stay over at Dylan's. Mrs. Ryder has me stay in the guest room but as soon as she is asleep, I always sneak over to Dylan's room to hang out with him. It is during these precious nights that we go on our most secretive adventures. Tonight, is our boldest one yet. We wait until after dark and can hear Mrs. Ryder's soft snoring before grabbing sweaters and flashlights. Dylan brings bear spray too because—of course—he does. Even at twelve years old, he looks out for me.

As soon as Dylan signals that we are in the clear, we slide out the back door and make a run for it. The moon is full tonight and there is not a cloud in sight. After our eyes adjust, we can see even without the use of our flashlights. We never stop to take a breath, we just run. We know we have limited time because if Mrs. Ryder wakes up and we are gone, there will be hell to pay.

We have been planning this for weeks, we wanted to be sure we were ready and that it would be the perfect night to do this. Dylan was worried about getting caught in a rainstorm, so he made us wait for a clear night. He also needed time to find the perfect carving instrument. He found one: his father's antique pocketknife—the one with the leather handle.

Finally, we make it. While gasping for breath, Dylan leans against the boulder and asks, "Are you sure about where you want it?"

"Yes," *I take another moment to catch my breath,* "put it right on top, in between where we sit. That way we'll always see it."

Dylan pulls out the pocketknife and looks to me, "Okay, hold the light."

For the first time tonight, I turn on my flashlight. I knew it would work because Dylan checked it before we left. It was all part of the planning. I turn it towards the boulder and Dylan climbs up. Once he is settled, he starts carving.

"How long will this take? We have to hurry, Dyl."

"Not long. This knife is sharp. It'll be quick."

We could have done this during the day. We are at this boulder all the time, in fact, we were here earlier today looking it over to decide on a spot to carve into it. We come at night, though, because it is one of our adventures and adventures are always more dangerous in the dark. We have wanted to come up here at night for years, but our parents never let us. It can be dangerous because of wild animals, and they worry we could get lost or hurt.

Swoosh. Thud.

"Dyl, what's that?" *I whisper scream.*

Dylan pulls out the bear spray and holds it out in front of him, waiting for something to come up to us but nothing does.

"Hurry, Dyl! Hurry!"

He turns and quickly finishes the carving before we hear another swoosh, *then turns to me with a panic-stricken face and says,* "May—run."

We run, and fast. Faster than we ever have. Once we are back in the safety of the house, we race to his bedroom and shut the door, sliding down on the other side of it panting and breathing so hard I have to clutch my chest.

"That was a close one, Dyl. We were almost eaten by somethin'!"

"I know, I know. But don't worry. I'd never have let it get you."

I smile before saying, "I know," because I did. I reach over and grab Dylan's hand in mine, squeezing it as I do.

He looks at me and smiles before squeezing back and says, "Wow, that was fun."

I have always had a hard time describing Dylan to my friends back home in Vermont. I tell them I have a best friend who I see only in the summers, but they don't understand. They ask me what he's like and I struggle to find the right words. Nothing I say ever seems to convey just how wonderful he really is. It isn't until right now, with his eyes on mine, out of breath from another amazing adventure, that I know how I will describe him from now on. I tell him, because I want him to know, too.

"Dyl?"

"Yeah?"

"If a sunflower was a person, it'd be you." *He smiles one of his biggest smiles, his dimple at its deepest. He smiles because he understands just how much I love the sunflowers.*

The memory is so loud in my head, I wonder for a moment if Dylan can hear it, too. I brave a peek at his face, nervous for what I might see. He appears lost in thought, chewing on his bottom lip and staring out at the view. His jaw ticks and I know he caught me looking at him so I quickly turn away.

After a quick lunch of granola bars and beef jerky, I ask for a few more moments of rest before we get back to looking for Sally. Dylan looks at me with surprise but agrees.

An undiscernible amount of time goes by—a few minutes turn into a few more and we find ourselves doing what we always did as kids—making our way to the sunflowers and laying amongst them. We do this without speaking as if our bodies are operating on muscle memory alone.

The sunflowers are swaying above me in the breeze—their petals fluttering slightly. The sun is illuminating them, and the blue of the sky is soft overhead. I'm enjoying the view so much that I actively ignore the couple of small ants that have crawled onto my arm and the storm clouds that are inching closer by the second.

Memories continue to fill the crevices in my mind, bleeding through the cracks in the walls I have built.

"Do you think we'll be friends forever?" I ask this already knowing the answer.

"Definitely."

"Do you think you'll ever hate me?" Dylan has his eyes shut and his arms crossed behind his head. We have been here all day, but the sun is starting to go down and our time here is running out.

"Impossible."

"Wouldn't you rather be best friends with a boy?"

"Why? Would you rather be best friends with a girl?"

"No way." The truth is, I can't image being best friends with anybody who was not Dylan Ryder. I look down at the cast on my arm. This is the first time since I broke it that I have been able to come back to the sunflower field and I have missed it so much. The only signature I have on it is from Dylan in blue ink. It reads:

Get well soon DORK, Love Dylan. Dylan always either calls me dork or May and I do not mind either. In fact, I really love May, and now it's what everyone calls me.

According to my mom, the nickname began when I was eight. It came naturally, and I don't even really know how it happened, but one day Dylan started calling me May. I think it was because I was obsessed with the month of May. It's my favorite month—it's the month that I come here.

I hear Dylan approaching, the rustling drawing closer, pulling me out of the memory. "Miranda? Where are you?" Dylan peels back two of the sunflowers and stands over me, the sun lighting up the left side of his face. The side of his mouth lifts slightly indicating an almost smile and a burning sensation lights up my skin. *Must be the sunburn.*

"There you are. We should get moving. If we head northeast, we might be able to beat the storm."

I roll my eyes, "You were always the responsible one." I laugh as I say this because it's true. Dylan was the one who made sure I had a sweater when we were out past dark, or who would give me his if I needed it. He was the one who made sure we would stop to eat lunch, and the one who was careful to get me home in time for dinner so that my parents would not worry.

"Wow, you laughed. That's the first time I've heard you laugh since we were fourteen. You should do it more often." Instead of urging me to get up, Dylan shocks me by easing his body down beside me, propping his head up on one arm. Are the sunflowers starting to work their magic after all?

"I used to laugh all the time."

"What happened?" He is close enough that I can smell his cologne—a mix of pine and campfire. Of course, that is the scent he would wear. It is so . . . him.

"My life fell apart." Apparently, the sunflowers are working their magic on me by making me weirdly honest.

"What do you mean? You've got a great life. I thought you liked college and all that."

"Actually, I got kicked out of college." *Okay*, maybe sunflowers are just truth serum.

"What? I'm sorry, I didn't know that."

"And a DUI. But it was dropped to reckless driving." *Oh. My. Gosh.* Someone please tell me to shut up.

"Wow . . . you know it'll be okay, May. You're still young. You can turn it around. Why didn't you tell me? Why'd you lie about it at dinner the other night?"

"I was embarrassed, obviously. I didn't want you—I mean your mom—to think less of me."

"You care what I think of you?" *Darn*, I was hoping he did not catch the slip up.

I roll my eyes, "Duh. I consider you a great friend." I say this with a sarcastic smile hoping he will drop it.

"Hm. You normally lie to your friends?" I open my mouth to respond but nothing comes out. "May, I just don't think we need to pretend to be something we aren't. We're not friends anymore. We haven't been for years. I told you I forgive you, and I do, but that doesn't mean we can go back to the way we were." As he speaks, casually, as though the words were not smashing my heart to bits, I cannot help but watch the way his mouth moves. He really is beautiful.

I take a deep breath, desperate not to cry again. "I know, Dylan. But maybe we can at least be friend-*ly*, maybe not like before, but more than we are now?"

"Why do you want to be friends with me? Let me guess, you feel guilty about ghosting me, so you just want to make yourself feel better?"

The truth in his words cuts me like a sword. He's

right. I do feel guilty. A deep and unexpected thought surfaces: *It's more than that. I want to be more than friends.* Where did that come from? I lecture myself silently.

"May—I mean Miranda. Am I right? You just want to rid your guilt?" His face is crinkled between his brows, his annoyance is palpable.

"So, what if that is part of it? That doesn't mean I also don't want us to be friends again. I mean, I've missed you." The words are out before I can stop them. It is as though my mouth and brain are no longer connected. I know myself well and, right now, I assure you that I am blushing. *Hard.* All I can do is hope that the sunburn conceals it.

"You've missed me?" I make the mistake of making eye contact. Dylan's eyes are wide, his pupils are dilated, and his jaw is clenched.

"Of course," I say with a soft smile and a shrug.

Dylan bites his lip, making a facial expression that reminds me of desire, but I know that's not possible so it must be something else.

A few beats go by, and Dylan plucks the stem of a small white flower that is in the space between our bodies. "Here," he says this softly as he tucks the stem behind my ear. "There, just like how you used to do it."

The fact that he remembers that I used to put wildflowers in my hair does something to me that is hard to explain. In a way, it makes me nervous. It makes this reunion with him, and this place, all too real.

His hand just grazes the skin of my ear, but the sensation causes desire to ping inside my abdomen. What is going on with my body? Am I seriously so attracted to Dylan Ryder that small touch on my ear would illicit a response? Why am I reacting this way to him?

I suddenly feel the urge to run so I look for a quick

getaway, "We need to go. I can smell the rain."

"Yeah, me too." Dylan seems nervous now too, he must sense my energy.

We sprint to take shelter by our boulder as the storm cuts loose. It's coming in fast.

Thunder erupts causing me to yelp out a cry, which only makes Dylan laugh as he says, "Come on! Run faster!"

"I'm trying! Don't laugh at me!"

We finally make it and quickly tuck ourselves beside our boulder.

"We should have left forty minutes ago! We could have beat this!" Dylan is yelling over the thunder.

"My fault!"

Dylan pulls his hoodie back out from his backpack and creates a makeshift umbrella for us to sit under.

We are both panting, the run draining our energy. The rain begins to pour down in sheets, the dark clouds are hovering over us, only allowing the sun to peek through for a few seconds at a time. I scoot into the nook under his arm for shelter and I can feel the warmth of his body through his t-shirt. The sweater does little against the downpour and soon cool water is drenching us.

I notice that we are both still panting long after we have stopped running. I begin to wonder if what is causing me to lose my breath, is causing him to lose his.

I tilt my head back slightly so that I can look into his eyes only to instantly regret it. His eyes are on me—melting me in swirls of caramel and velvet. His jaw line is tight, and his lips are parted as he takes in ragged breath after ragged breath.

It dawns on me that I want him to kiss me. In fact, I'm *desperate* for it. I place my left hand on the back of his wet hair and inch his face slowly down towards mine.

Dylan bites his bottom lip and does not resist as I begin to draw him closer, but then—abruptly—he stops. He pulls his head back out of my grasp and looks at me with wild eyes.

"I can't." He voice is so low that I almost think I imagined it, but the look in his eyes assures me I didn't.

"Oh—Okay, sorry." My head is swimming now with shame and embarrassment. My hand is hot from where I touched him. I can't believe I just tried to kiss Dylan Ryder and he rejected me.

I will never be able to recover from this moment.

Chapter Fourteen

Dylan

My phone vibrates in my pocket, drawing me back to reality and just in the nick of time.

Oh no. What am I doing? It takes every ounce of energy I can gather to utter two words I never dreamed I would say to Miranda Carlson.

"I can't."

I said it as a form of self-preservation. Did I *want* to say it? God, no. Did I want to lose myself in kissing her? God, yes.

She looks at me with big, sparkling eyes making it even harder to pull away.

"Okay, sorry." Her cheeks flush and she bites down on her bottom lip, and I can tell she is embarrassed. My gut is twisting now—crying out in agony. I should be *thrilled.* I have the ultimate payback, the ultimate revenge to be able to turn down the girl who broke my heart. I should—but I don't. No, there is nothing thrilling about this moment, just the desperate need to get away.

"We'd better get back to looking for Sally." My chest is so tight, the words struggle to find air.

What have I done?

Did I really almost kiss May? And in the rain like in the damn movies?!

Crap, I'm in trouble. Do I tell Candace? I know I should, but I really do not want to. Maybe I do not need to tell her since nothing actually happened.

These thoughts race through my head as we spend the

rest of the afternoon hiking farther up the mountain in silence.

"Dylan, I admit it. I'm exhausted. Do you think we should head back down the mountain? I'm sorry about Sally, but maybe she will turn up back at the ranch. Should we call your mom and see if she wants us to keep looking?"

"I can't, my phone died hours ago. Plus, even if I had power, we wouldn't get reception up this far . . . but you're right, we need to stop and rest. We won't make it back down this mountain before dark, though."

"Oh. What do we do then?" May looks at me with a whisper of uncertainty in her eyes.

"I brought a small pop-up tent in my backpack. I'll set it up for you."

"You did?"

"Yeah, my mom made me bring it just in case we would have trouble finding Sally. We need to find an open area with flat ground. Follow me for just a few more minutes." I lead May to a small grassy area just outside the tree line and on the banks of the creek. It's the flattest area and the farthest I can get us away from the trees.

"While you do that, what can I do to help?"

"Gather some small branches for me to use for kindling. I'll make a fire when I have this tent up."

Thirty minutes later, the tent is up, and a small fire is going despite the wet ground thanks to my mom reminding me to pack the Firestarter. May is sitting on my backpack beside me while I'm on the grassy terrain. I would have used my hoodie, but I gave it to May. She, *of course*, did not bring one and is cold the second the sun drops below the horizon. Some things never change.

The crackling fire is all that can be heard now. There is no wind and even the leaves on the trees have gone quiet. The almost kiss from earlier is at the forefront of my mind and while the world outside my head is quiet, the one inside my head is screaming. I do not know what is going on with May and me, but I'm not about to open that door. The last time I gave her my heart, she stomped all over it.

"Dylan, about earlier. I'm sorry if I made you uncomfortable. I shouldn't have tried to kiss you. I don't know what I was thinking." I should be glad she is trying to clear the air, but it only makes my stomach twist more. I have to say something, I have to put a stop to whatever this is.

"It's okay. Let's just forget it." I sigh deeply before continuing. Here goes, "We can try to be friendly with each other and that's fine, but I don't want anything more than that. It's not possible for me to get close to you again after what happened when we were fourteen. I just . . . can't. Sorry." Wow, that was even harder to say than I expected.

"I understand." I don't look in her direction, I don't want to see her face right now for fear I might change my mind.

"Can I ask you something, Dylan?"

"I guess so."

"What did you write me?"

"What?"

"You wrote me letters, but I never read them. What did they say?"

I pause before responding to try to gather myself, "Uh. I dunno'. That was so long ago. Probably just embarrassing stuff. I'm relieved you never read them. I hope you threw them in the trash instead."

"Just so you know, I didn't do it to hurt you. I did it to protect me." I glance at her before turning back to the fire, regretting it. Her face looks pained, reminding me of how she looked the day she broke her arm and I have to bite down on the inside of my cheek to stop myself from throwing my arms around her. Say *something,* Dylan—anything.

I open my mouth, but nothing comes out.

Chapter Fifteen

Miranda

At least I tried.

I tried to repair our broken relationship, but I have to accept that this cannot be fixed. The past and the hurt I have caused Dylan is too much for him to overcome. We will never be anything more than friendly acquaintances and I need to learn to be okay with that. My guilt from what I did to him may never fade entirely but I must find a way to accept this.

As I *try* to convince myself that I can be okay with the way things are between us, the light from the fire dances along the surface on my tent creating an enchanting view transporting me back to the magic I believed in as a child. Missing my childlike wonder, my head swarms with the fairies, mystical beings and secret worlds that used to fill me with such joy.

I shake my head to erase the thoughts from my mind, reminding myself that it's not magic. Just the flames of a fire that is too close to my tent.

Pulling the sleeves of Dylan's gray hoodie up over my fingertips to warm my now very cold body, I try to visualize what Dylan is doing on the other side of this thin fabric. How is he possibly going to sleep out there on the cold, hard ground? I consider telling him he can sleep in here with me but after the almost kiss earlier, I'm pretty sure he would think I was just trying to make a pass at him. Which I am not—*obviously*.

Unable to force sleep to come, and with Dylan's presence infiltrating every cell of my body, it's impossible for memories of us not to filter into my consciousness. For a moment—just a brief one—I allow myself to revel in them.

We always climb trees.

There is not a day that goes by that we don't.

We have our favorites—the one closest to Dylan's house that I used to climb onto his roof being mine. The other is the one near our boulder. It is the only one that is an aspen tree instead of a pine, so it has a white trunk that makes it particularly beautiful. It also has a great branch to sit on that provides an awesome view of the sunflower field—second only to the boulder, so it's hard not to like.

Today, we decide to conquer the biggest one we have found. The big, and probably very old, pine off the north side of the Ryder ranch, near where Sally and the other horses spend their afternoons running.

We have never climbed this one before. Mrs. Ryder has insisted that we don't. She says it is too big and easy to get stuck on, but we feel particularly invincible today and Mrs. Ryder is in town picking up supplies, so she will never have to know.

Dylan and I are standing at the base of the big tree, heads tilted all the way back in attempt to assess just how tall this bad boy is. Dylan is only about an inch shorter than me, but it's enough that I take on the role of "the tall one."

"Okay, Dylan, it's tall, but I think we can handle it. I can see some great climbing branches from here." I point up to a specific branch that has caught my eye.

"I'll go first, May. I'm going to see how far up I can get, then you can follow me."

"No, Dylan. I'm taller than you. It's better if I go first." At thirteen, we were both very focused on who was taller and stronger.

"May, you're a girl. You might be a little taller, but I'm definitely stronger."

"No way, Dyl." I walk up to the trunk and begin to

grab the base so I can scoot myself up to the first branch.

"Whatever. Be careful, May, and hurry up. My mom will be so mad if she sees us."

"She'll be gone at least two hours, we'll be fine." I am already onto branch number two now.

To be a good tree climber, there are a few things you must do. First, make sure you have tennis shoes on and that the shoelaces are tied. Second, make sure you are not tired and have a lot of energy. The last thing you want to do is climb up only to run out of enough energy to climb back down. Third, always have someone with you in case something goes wrong. With our expert climbing skills, Dylan and I never think we could get hurt climbing the big tree. It's not until I am up about halfway and my shoe slips, leaving me grasping my arms around a branch, that we start to think we may be in over our heads.

My arms are wrapped around the now creaking tree branch, my careful avoidance of pine needles no longer in play as my arms grip tighter and needles dig into my bare arms.

"May! Hang on! I'm coming!"

I'm careful not to move around much as I listen to Dylan racing up the tree underneath me, but I'm beginning to panic. It's a hot day and the sun is high and I have a layer of sweat making my grip slippery.

Dylan is a couple of feet under me now, I turn my head so I can see the top of his. I think he is going to get to me before I fall but that changes in an instant.

It happens so fast that I don't have time to think. The next thing I know, I'm lying on the ground on top of my right arm. I can hear Dylan and I think he's screaming my name.

The memory of breaking my arm should not be a fond

one but for some inexplicable reason, I smile. It's probably because the next thing I remember after the fall is little Dylan carrying me as he ran towards the house. As I looked up at him, too shocked to feel the pain yet, I remember seeing his face scrunched and red and sweating.

He glanced down at my face briefly and said something that made me realize everything was going to be okay. "I've got you, May."

That's the thing about Dylan. He always had me. He was always there for me. He would never have done to me what I did to him. He was always the better friend—the better person. Another memory pushes forward as these thoughts consume me.

"May—it's okay. We'll still see each other a ton."

I'm twelve years old, and this year has been my worst ever. My body changed in a dramatic way which is why I "have emotions that can be hard to understand," at least according to my mother. I'm on the phone crying to Dylan because I found out that for the first time since I was six years old, I will not be going to the mountain in May. We have to wait until the first week of June because my mom is contracted with a big interior design job, and she will not be done with the project until June.

She does not understand how upsetting this is. After having an awful year of hating some of my teachers, being teased for having to wear braces, and getting my period which has led to the development of pimples, the only thing I had to look forward to was getting to the mountain and hanging out with my best friend. Now, thanks to my ridiculous mother, I'm forced to wait another three weeks before going. I just can't catch a break.

I'm devastated. I cried all day today after I got the

news. I called Dylan as soon as I knew he was home because he always knows what to say when I'm upset like this.

We have always talked and wrote each other letters during the school years but this year has been different. I have needed him more, so I have called and wrote more than I ever have. You would think he might get tired of me, but he never does. He always sounds thrilled when I call, and he started calling me more, too. It's kind of weird having a best friend that you don't see during the school year, but it has always been like this, so I think we are just kind of used to it.

"Dyl, I won't be on the mountain until June. My name is MAY." I say this incredulously because he is not understanding what a big deal this is.

"It's one summer. It sucks bad 'cause I'm going to be miserable waiting for you, but it's just one summer. We have summers for the rest of our lives to spend together, three weeks is not a big deal." He always says the right things, calming me instantly. My dad calls him a "miracle worker."

"Will you get a new best friend?" I know he would never, but I need to hear it.

"Of course not, May. I don't want to be best friends with anyone else."

I smile to myself and wipe my eyes, but the tears have stopped. "You really think we'll spend summers together for the rest of our lives?"

"Obviously."

"What if we changed or got married or had kids or somethin'?"

"No matter what happens, I'll always be your best friend and I'll always spend my summers on this ranch and when I'm grown-up, I'll be out of school and will be here year-round. So as long as you keep coming here, I'll *be here waiting for you." I smile again. He really does know the right thing to say.*

Thanks to the trip down memory lane, stress and guilt drench my body in discomfort causing my skin to prick with pain. Dylan was always there for me, comforting me and supporting me no matter what and I dropped him—without a single word.

My whole body shakes with a sudden and desperate need for a drink.

A distant howl forces me to wake from an uncomfortable slumber. My neck is kinked with tension and my brows are scrunched as I open my eyes. *Was that a wolf?* There are plenty of bears and wolves up in these mountains, so I'm not surprised. Generally speaking, they leave you alone but when you are out here with no protection, it's hard not to get a little spooked.

I wonder if Dylan heard that.

I slowly unzip the tent just enough to peek out and see Dylan sitting by the now smoking embers. I cannot tell if his eyes are shut but I assume not since I don't see how anyone could sleep sitting up.

"Dylan?" I whisper just in case the wolves are listening.

"Yeah?" Dylan does not whisper back. Apparently, he is not as worried about the wolves as I am.

"Can you not sleep?"

"No, it's too hard to. I figured I would just stay awake until the sun came up."

"Did you hear the howling?"

"Yup."

"Did it scare you?"

"No. Why, did it scare you?"

"No, course not." Lies.

"It's okay. They'll leave us alone. I have bear spray in case anything actually comes for us."

"Oh, good . . ." I debate about what I want to say next. "Dylan, don't take this as me making a pass at you, but you can sleep in here. There's room."

"I'm okay out here."

"But it's safer in here."

"Are you telling me that you think a thin piece of fabric is going to protect us from wolves and bears?"

"No, but I dunno. Maybe." He is definitely taking this the wrong way. "I won't touch you, Dylan. Plus, there's a blanket in here we can share. You have to be cold out here."

There is a long pause. *Too* long. My mortification at my constant states of humiliation today is really becoming too much.

"Fine, stay out there and freeze then."

"Okay, okay. Geez."

Dylan comes over and finishes unzipping the tent. The very small space is a tight fit for two people. I shove my body over to one side completely in a desperate attempt to give him some room to lay down without touching him. I never realized just how massive he is until this moment. He must be at least six foot two.

He manages to lay down next to me and crosses his arms over this chest, clearly not wanting to risk his hand or arm coming to close to me. The level of discomfort bunched up in here is so thick, you couldn't cut through it with the sharpest of knives.

"Breathe."

"What?"

"You're holding your breath." *Damn*, he's right. I do

as I'm told and ragged breaths force their way in and out of my lungs. "You're being so weird."

"Really? I am? And laying like a mummy is how you normally sleep?"

"Okay, fine." Dylan pulls his arms out of the crossed position and places them straight by his side.

"*Muuuch* better."

"Shut up. Obviously, this is uncomfortable. I'm never going to be able to sleep like this." A thought occurs to me that might help. Something that I picked up in college—an icebreaker.

"Maybe we can break the tension by playing a game?"

"What game?"

"Truth or dare?"

"If you think it'll help." His doubt at this being a good idea drips off each syllable with sticky sarcasm.

"Give it a chance. I'll go first. Truth or dare?"

"Uhh . . . dare."

"Hmm, I dare you to moo like a cow for thirty seconds." One thing I learned in college was that icebreakers always help ease tension, but you can't take them too seriously.

"Really? That's my dare?"

"Were you hoping for something more dangerous?"

"Moooooo . . ." Dylan moos for a solid thirty seconds and the muscles in my face are tight as I try not to burst out in laughter.

"Okay, my turn. Truth or dare."

"Dare."

"I dare you to quack like a duck for sixty seconds."

"I knew you'd say something like that."

"Get started, I'll time you."

I start quacking and it's the longest minute of my life, made longer by Dylan's laughing at me. "And I thought mooing was embarrassing."

"Whatever, truth or dare?"

"I guess truth this time."

"What did you say in those letters?" This might be the only chance I get to find out, so I jump at the chance to find out.

"Pass."

"Passing is not an option."

"I really don't want to go there Ma—Miranda."

"Dylan, please. Just give me some idea and I'll never mention it again for the rest of our lives."

Dylan does not say anything for a long time. I can tell I am crossing a line, but I just have to know what he wrote to me. "It's embarrassing, I can't. I pass. We each get one pass, okay?"

He turns his head slightly towards me, a streak of moonlight coming in from the small hole at the top of the tent glides over his eye, resembling a long scar running down his face—creating an intimidating image. A shiver runs down my spine—vibrating my heart as it does.

"Okay, fine. I'll drop it. We each get one pass." I will ask something a bit safer so that he keeps playing the game. "How many girlfriends have you had?"

"Hmm. . . a few. What counts as a girlfriend?"

"Someone you called your girlfriend at least once and you had to have at least kissed." Mentioning kissing might not be my best move because Dylan flinches at the word.

"Um, well I guess four then."

"Wow, that's a lot."

"Is it? Why, how many boyfriends have you had?"

"Two. One in high school and one in college. I was never very serious with either, though."

Dylan nods and opens his mouth like he wants to stay something more, but shuts it quickly as he changes his mind.

"Truth or dare?"

"Isn't it my turn?"

"You used your turn when you asked me how many boyfriends I've had."

"We did not establish that. I wouldn't have asked if I knew I'd lose a turn."

"Okay, fine. Truth."

"What was in that tin we found buried in the yard?"

Damn him. "Pass."

"Pass? Really?"

"You said we each get one."

"Okay, fine. I'll ask something else. Did it have anything to do with me?"

I take my time in responding. I have already used my pass and if I want to keep him talking to me, I better respond. "Okay, yes. It did have something to do with you, but not all of it was about you."

"Huh, ok. How very cryptic of you."

"I know. Your turn. Truth or dare?"

"Truth."

Taking a deep breath, I decide to be brave and ask the questions that my head wants to know, but I'm not so sure my heart can handle. "When did you lose your virginity?"

I hold my breath waiting for the answer. If I was honest with myself, I hate that it wasn't with me. On some level, even as kids, I always figured all of my firsts would be with Dylan. My first hike, my first swim, my first horseback ride, my first crush, my first kiss. It was always Dylan—all my firsts. *Until it wasn't.* Until I threw that away for someone else to have the rest of my firsts.

I can tell Dylan does not want to answer. I also know that it is because he probably also always thought it would be with me. He sighs, but ultimately gives in. "It was with a girl named Mariah."

"Oh, that's a pretty name." Lies—I hate her and the name.

"Yeah. I was eighteen and she was my first serious girlfriend. I had another girlfriend before her, but we never had sex."

"How'd it happen?"

"I don't know, really. It just did. She came over to my grandparents' place after class one day while they were both still at the store working, so we were alone. I think we both knew what we were there for. I wish I could say it was an awesome experience but it was more awkward than anything. It was very fast and I don't even think I got my pants all the way off. It took us some time before we got the hang of it and it was actually enjoyable." The thought of him having enjoyable sex with anyone causes a wave of nausea to suddenly strike. I swallow heavily before asking the next question.

"Why'd you break up?"

"She left for college. She wanted to be single while she was there."

"Were you heartbroken?"

"No, May. I wasn't. I have only ever had my heart broken once and I don't plan on ever letting that happen again." Of course, I know that he is talking about me but I do not say anything more about it, not wanting him to shut down and stop talking to me.

"What about you?"

"What about me?"

"Your virginity?" I should have seen this question coming. I should have known he might ask. Still, I'm not prepared for it. My heart is beating in a painful way now, like it's out of rhythm. Sweat has formed along the back of my neck despite the cool nighttime air.

"Pass." The hitch in my voice betrays me, and Dylan hears it immediately.

"You already used your pass."

"I know, but I can't answer that question. Ask me another one, please?"

"What's wrong, May? Did something happen?"

"No. No," I need to change the subject quickly, "I just don't want to talk about it. It's not an interesting story."

Dylan's face is turned towards me and his brows are pulled together in concern. I can see that he wants to push, but I give him a look that I hope conveys a combination of *it's no big deal* and *just drop it*. Dylan hesitates—a million questions cross his face but he never says anything. He knows me well enough to know when I'm done talking about something, so he does not push, but I can tell by the tightness in his face that he's not happy about it.

"Go on, ask me something else."

He signs, "Okay. Hmmm . . . how have you celebrated the rest of your birthdays?"

What he doesn't know, is that this is another very uncomfortable topic. What he does not know is that I have not celebrated my birthday in three years. He cannot know, I do not want him to know—so I lie.

"Oh, just the usual. Have a party with friends. No horseback riding, though."

"Bummer. Bonfires?"

"Always." I smile a fake smile because this is also a lie. I have not been to a bonfire since my fourteenth birthday here on this very mountain.

Desperate to get away from these questions, I throw it all out there into the universe. "Truth or Dare?"

"Truth."

"Do you ever think about me?" It is a dangerous question but I have already embarrassed myself so profoundly today, I might as well embrace it.

With his head still turned towards me, my heart is

beating so loud I worry he can see it pounding against the cloth of this now sweaty hoodie.

He takes his time to answer, and when he does it's a soft, "Yes."

It's a simple word, yes. Most days it means nothing significant. We probably say it a dozen times every day and it bears little meaning. But this yes, this single yes, is something different. Something that can only be described as *powerful*.

With his eyes still fixed on mine, he dives over the edge with me, "Truth or dare?"

"Truth." It's barely a whisper now.

"Do you ever think about—"

"Yes." The word escapes my lips before I can use my last few brain cells to think about what I'm saying. Dylan bites his lower lip and bunches up his dark eyebrows. A flash of uncertainty and something else glimmers across his face, perhaps pain. It's too brief for me to know for sure.

"This is a mistake." His voice is harsh now like it hurts to speak.

"I know." And I do know. This is definitely a mistake. If we kiss right now, our relationship will be forever changed—just as it was after our first kiss.

Dylan slowly lifts his right hand and uses his thumb to sweep across my jaw and over my bottom lip. Nerves wreck me—my stomach filling in with knots and my hands are almost violently shaking. I have kissed boys before, there is no logical reason for me to be this nervous, but this is no ordinary boy.

"You're trembling," he says this delicately before lifting his head and using his hand to lightly lift my chin. I shut my eyes in anticipation and wait quietly to feel his lips on mine. An eternity later, nothing is happening and my lonely lips begin to worry. Opening my eyes, I see

Dylan looking at me with an array of emotions splayed across his beautiful face.

I can no longer take it.

I lift my head up before he can stop me and plant my mouth on his. He gasps in surprise. I press on, opening my mouth and running my tongue along the seam of his lips, encouraging him to let me in to get a better taste. Reluctantly, Dylan opens his mouth just enough for me to gain access. He is warm and wonderful, tasting of red Gatorade and the fruit roll up I saw him eat earlier by the fire.

Even though he is letting me taste him, he is not reciprocating and I'm suddenly overcome with regret, pulling back and turning a deep shade of red. I'm just grateful it's too dark in this tent for him to see.

He hesitates before placing his hand on the back of my head and bringing me back to him, this time dipping his tongue into my mouth.

I wish I could say it was awful.

I wish I could say that my skin does not tingle all over my body from the simple and small movement of his tongue caressing mine, but I can't. I can't say any of it.

Too soon, though, he pulls away.

"May—I can't. I'm sorry. I just can't."

Chapter Sixteen

Dylan

I must be losing it.

There is no other explanation. I'm attracted to the one girl who completely destroyed me. I used to consider myself a rational man, but after the tent debacle I'm beginning to question if I have any brain cells at all.

Even though it was only for a few seconds, I got a taste of her and she tasted good. *Too good.* And now those few seconds are ruining my life. It's all I think about. *For days.* All night it haunts my dreams, all day it distracts my every thought.

After we separated ourselves from each other's lips, May turned onto her side so that her back was towards me. I know it was because she did not want me to see her face and I hate to think it might have been because she was crying. It only took about ten minutes before I knew I could not stay in there with her, as I have never felt such a heavy tension in my entire life. The air in the space around us was so thick, it was hard to breathe. Under the weight of near suffocation, I got up slowly and exited the tent without a word. There was nothing that I could say. I *wanted* to say that I was sorry again, but I couldn't bring myself to say anything more.

The next morning, we managed to make it back down the mountain without incident. We were kind of normal towards each other and had some small talk about the weather and some friends we used to know as kids. It was far from normal, though. I never once made eye contact—I couldn't. I was so worried she would see right through me if I did.

When we got back to my ranch, I was shocked to see Sally. Apparently, she came home on her own sometime in the night. This crazy horse—and my mother—must be plotting against me.

That was three days ago and I'm still overwhelmed with all things May. Desperate to get past the kiss, I spent the last hour in the horse barn going crazy on the punching bag I have hanging from the rafters, trying to punch my way out of thinking about her. It is here that I also decide not to tell Candace about any of it.

I know. *I know.*

It's probably not the right call, or *technically* the right thing to do, but hear me out. Candance is coming here—soon. The rest of this summer would be too awkward for everyone involved if I tell her now before she and her family embark on this non-refundable trip.

I do not want to lose Candace. I just need to shake these feelings towards May and focus on my perfect girlfriend.

As long as I do not die from a stress induced stroke, I should be okay.

Right?

Chapter Seventeen

Miranda

My mother arrives with the tenants today and I have everything ready. I just hope she is impressed. I have been such a disappointment that I want to show her I can do something right, but the guilt of my drinking her wine sits heavy in my stomach, reminding me that there is nothing for her to be proud of.

I have managed to avoid Dylan for the last few days. Which proves not to be difficult thanks to him actively avoiding me, as well. The night in the tent almost gave me an aneurysm—knocking every morsel of wind out of my body leaving me completely breathless . . . and stupid. He rejected me. *Repeatedly*. There has never been a person on this planet who has ever been more embarrassed than me. He has the upper hand. I gave it to him on a silver platter and I just look like the pathetic girl who is obsessed with kissing him.

I *must* end this. I must regain control of this situation. I cannot leave this place with him thinking I am as pathetic as I am.

But how?

I grab a pen and jot down my plan:

How to regain my dignity in four simple steps:

1-Avoid Dylan at all costs.
2-If you see him, ignore him completely.
3-If he tries to talk to you, pretend you speak another language.
4-Lastly, and most importantly, NEVER kiss him again.

Yup, fool proof plan. Genius. Impeccable. No problems here.

After some last-minute dusting, I put on my most grown up and professional looking blazer and sit on the porch to wait for their arrival.

The silence of the mountains surrounds me while I wait.

Silence in the mountains does not mean no sound at all—you can still hear plenty. You can hear the leaves on the trees swaying in the breeze and the cooing of the birds flying overhead. Silence in the mountains is in what you don't hear: people, traffic, dogs barking, children playing. It's what most people would call peaceful.

The problem with it, though, is that it allows for painful memories and long ignored thoughts to be heard. My heart rate begins to increase as memories flood my brain. A flash of my parents dancing in the living room while I watched them from the staircase forces its way into my mind's eye. They thought I was asleep, but I had come down the stairs to grab a drink and stopped when I saw my dad twirling my mom around with the glow from the fireplace blazing behind them, coating the image of them in a warm light. You would think it was strange that they would dance without any music, but—somehow—it was not. They did not need music, because they had each other.

I shake the image from my head, feeling betrayed. How could they divorce when they seemed so in love? They rarely ever fought, they were always smiling at each other, and they would steal moments like these to be alone together. They never explained why they divorced.

The only thing my mother has ever said was "sometimes people just grow apart and there's nothing they can do about it." This always sounded like a non-answer to me, but oh well. It does not really matter. No matter the why—they split—forever proving to me that love is not real.

My heart is racing inside my chest. I need to refocus my thoughts and calm my heartbeat before I have a full-blown panic attack. The sun is still low and the breeze is cool, causing goosebumps to pop up along my arms. It's so hard to be surrounded by the beauty of this place and to not regret that I have stayed away from here for so long. The sting of regret is now pooling inside my chest, further increasing my heart rate and making it harder and harder to breathe. My hands begin to go numb and I start pacing around the porch in an attempt to force myself to shake off these feelings, but the sensation of drowning is consuming me.

Desperate to breathe, I run back into the house and barrel into the wine cellar. I gulp down a bottle of dry white wine so fast that I get an instant headache. Soon, the medicine works, though. My thoughts become cloudy and my body slows down, allowing oxygen into my lungs. I put the empty bottle back on the shelf hoping mom won't pick it up and notice that it is empty before I can replace it, and run upstairs to brush my teeth and rinse my mouth.

Swaying in front of the mirror in the bathroom, I recognize my terrible mistake.

Damn, what have I done? How am I going to hide this?

I stumble my way back out onto the porch, hoping the fresh air will get my head on straight, when I spot Dylan coming down the path causing the regret to combine with nervous energy. Of all the moments that I have to talk to

Dylan, this is the worst possible one. I need to get rid of him, and *quick*.

He has his hands tucked into his pockets and his eyebrows are scrunched together with worry as he steps onto the porch. I must be acting strangely so I force myself to sit on the porch swing to hide the swaying of my body. Trying to remember the list I made earlier, I think it best not to speak first.

Dylan leans back on the wooden post reminding me of a model in a magazine. "Hey."

"Heeyyyy." Crap, that came out sounding weird. "What're you doin' here?" Double crap, I slurred.

"Um . . . I need to tell you something." The pooling in my chest is now spilling over into the rest of my body.

"What?" I say this in a strange tone that does not even sound like my own voice.

"I just wanted to tell you something that I hadn't mentioned before, but thought you might want to know." He's stalling.

"Oh? What's that?" Hurry up and spit it out.

"Um, well the tenants that are staying at your place for the summer are the Winters from Boulder."

"Okay?"

"They are friends with my grandfather, and he told them all about the place, so they wanted to come."

"How do they know your grandfather?"

"They met him several times this last year because they would come by the store to pick up their daughter sometimes."

"Who's their daughter?"

"It's Candace, my girlfriend."

If hearts could explode from shock, mine would.

"Your girlfriend's parents are staying at my house? And her too?" The good thing about shock is it can sober you up in an instant.

"Um, yeah . . . sorry I didn't mention it sooner. I should've."

"Oh, okay." I don't know when it happened, but I am off the porch swing now and am pacing again.

"What's wrong? Why're you pacing around?"

"Nothing's wrong. But I do have a request." Everything is wrong. My body begins to shake.

"What?"

"Please don't have sex with her in this house, Dylan." I can feel the vein in my neck bulging, and I just hope he doesn't notice.

"What? Of course I won't. I wouldn't do that." At least he has the decency to look offended.

"I don't care—that you have sex with her." How do I save this? "Don't get me wrong, I would just be really grossed out if I heard you." Yeah, *great* save, Miranda.

"Sure, okay. I won't. We aren't animals and I definitely don't want you to hear us, either."

"Would you like it if you heard me?" What am I even *saying* right now?

"God, no." Dylan's petrified face calms me down a bit. At least it's not just me.

"Okay, then. We have an understanding."

"Sure." Dylan runs both hands through his hair as I force myself to appear relaxed enough to sit back down on the swing. "Can I wait here with you?"

"Free country."

"Okay, you seem pissed now."

"No, I'm not pissed . . . I just wasn't expecting that is all." I'm not mad, I have no right to be. At least this is what I keep telling myself.

"Okay. I get it."

Is he in love with her? Man, I want to know. *Damn*, this is not how I want to spend my summer.

"Miranda?"

"What?"

"Are you okay?"

"Why're you asking me that?" Can he tell I have been drinking? Am I still slurring my words?

"You just seem . . . off or something."

"I'm fine, Dylan." I snap at him hoping he takes a hint and shuts up. Of course, I don't get that lucky.

"Have you been drinking?"

Nooooo, if he can tell I have been drinking, how am I going to hide this from the tenants? My *mother*?

I must not respond quick enough because Dylan responds for me, "Miranda, what the hell is going on? Why have you been drinking at nine in the morning? Are you okay?"

He is kneeling in front of me now, speaking softly, as I put my head in my hands and lean forward so that my elbows are resting on my knees. Tears are flowing freely, soaking into the cuff of my blazer. I feel a warm hand on my shoulder, urging me to lift up.

"I'm so embarrassed, Dylan." This sentence is muffled by my hands.

"What's going on, May?" Dylan's voice is soft and low now, the childhood nickname bringing me comfort.

"I'm just really stressed is all. I'll be fine. Please don't say anything to anyone, okay? My mom can't know."

I must look pathetic because Dylan does not fight it, but nods slowly while chewing on his bottom lip in contemplation. "Is there anything I can do?"

How is it possible for him to care? After all that I have done to him, after how I treated him, how can he look at me with worry like he is right now? I do not deserve this from him and it makes my heart break even more.

"No, but thanks. Thank you for caring. I know I don't deserve it after what I did to you." My voice shakes thanks to my trembling body.

"May, don't talk like that. Of course, I care. How could I not? Why don't you go into the bathroom and clean up and make some coffee? I will wait out here for your mom and Candace."

"Okay, thanks, Dyl."

Chapter Eighteen

Dylan

I tell her about Candace, but that no longer seems important as I watch her cry into her hands.
What is going on?
Why is she drinking like this? She seems so miserable. She used to radiate joy and, now, it's like a dark cloud is always looming over her.

A blue Escalade followed by Lynn's silver Jeep come up the long drive. I should be thrilled to see my girlfriend, but a bundle of nerves is sitting in my chest causing my lungs to struggle. *I just hope that May is okay.* I shake the thought away immediately, *focus on your girlfriend, Dylan.*

The vehicle is barely in park before Candace is jumping out of the back and running in my direction. Her long blond hair and chest bounce as she hops up the steps and I feel a ping of guilt as she embraces me. I look back over my shoulder looking for May—hoping she did not see. For some inexplicable reason, even though she crushed me years ago, I do not actually have the desire to hurt her, especially after seeing her so upset. The thought disturbs me to the core.

"Hey, babyyy!" Candace says this as she finally removes her arms from around my neck.

"Hey, babe. Hello, Mr. Winters." I nod in the direction of Candace's dad. Mr. Winters nods back, but looks displeased. He is always looking at me like that though, so it's nothing new.

"Hello, Dylan, it's so great to see you, dear." Candace's mother says this as Domino pokes his head out of the top of her purse.

"Hey! It's great to see you, too." I glance over to

May's mother who looks the same as always. I have always liked her. "Hi Lynn, it's so nice to see you. It's been too long." I say this as she comes in for a side hug.

"Hi, Dylan. It has been a long time. How have you and Miranda been this summer? I wondered if you two were hanging out." Oh geez, not now Lynn, *please*.

"Uh, we're fine. I've seen her a little bit. Not much though." This comes out awkwardly, so I hope she gets the message and does not press for more in front of Candace.

"I didn't realize that Candace was your girlfriend until recently when your mother told me. That should be nice for you two to spend some time together here." I notice a hint of something off in her voice, like she doesn't really mean what she is saying.

"Hey, Mom, everything's ready. I can give the tenants a tour of the place if you like." May swoops in with the save and relief sweeps over my body.

"That'd be great, Miranda. You look lovely by the way."

I smile as I notice how May's face lights up at the compliment.

"Hello, I'm Candace." *Crap,* I forgot to introduce her.

"Hi, I'm Miranda. It's great to meet you. I hope you enjoy the place." The ice from May's voice could put frost on the sun but at least she seems composed. It's not obvious she's been drinking.

They all follow May into the house but I step back, pulling Candace with me. "Hey."

"Hey, baby," she says as she stands on her tiptoes and kisses me, "you comin' in?"

"No, I don't need a tour, I'll let you get settled. Call me when you wanna' come to my place."

"Okay." Candace heads inside after a quick kiss, leaving me to escape back to the ranch and far away from this awkward nightmare.

I used to believe that the passing of time was a blessing. Now, I know that the passing of time is actually a curse. It's the worst kind of curse, too, because it tricks you.

The passing of time tricked me into believing that I was over May. As the days wore on, I became accustomed to summers spent without her, to never hearing her laughter, to the emptiness I felt whenever someone used the phrase 'childhood friends' or 'first loves.' Now, I am beginning to understand that it was all an illusion. The years of friendship, the kiss, the pain of the unanswered phone calls and letters, have not gone away—*not at all*. Instead, they torment me as I lay here in bed with my arms wrapped around another woman.

I thought I was over this. I thought I had moved on.

I was tricked by the passage of time.

Chapter Nineteen

Miranda

The tenants are great.

Just *freaking* great.

Domino has become my nemesis. He is the *worst*. He is a tiny furry creature that chirps at me all day long and pees on the floor despite the special fence built outside just for his precious butt.

I know I should not take out my anger on a tiny, four-pound dog, but it is easier to be mad at Domino rather than Candace . . . or, worse, Dylan.

I wish I liked Candace; I wish we could be the best of friends. But seeing her wrap her long, perfectly spray tanned arms around Dylan's neck sent me into a jealous rage that I definitely did *not* see coming.

The feeling of jealously is unfamiliar to me as usually girls are jealous of me, not the other way around and, to be completely honest, I have never cared enough about anyone to be jealous over them. It is not a good look on me at all as, apparently, I'm quite petty when I'm jealous. For instance, Candace told me that she has to have bottled water and refuses to drink water out of the tap, even though the water here is delicious, so every time she leaves her pink water bottle laying around unattended, I pour it out and replace it with water from the sink. She also insists on eating organic blueberries daily as part of her 'special diet'. Her parents asked me to make weekly runs to town to make sure Candace never ran out of her organic blueberries so when I went to the store this week, I pulled the sticker off the organic ones and put in on the non-organic ones and gave those to her instead.

So, yeah, like I said, *petty*.

I have not even begun to try to make sense of why I

am so consumed with jealously, instead, I push it as far down into the dark corners of my brain as possible. I have spent this entire week lying to myself and pretending not to be bothered by the sight of them together and I like to think I'm doing a great job carrying on this little charade however, the nights spent crying into my pillow after a couple glasses of wine until I fall asleep seem to say different.

Today at noon, much to my horror, we are all meeting up at the hot spring just up Stony Creek path to the west of the Ryder Ranch. Dylan said Jebb and Diego will be joining us. I never liked them when I was a kid, but am hopeful that they are not as stupid now as they once were. The only reason I agreed to do this was because if I don't, I fear it will be too obvious that it is because I cannot handle seeing Dylan and Candace together and I'm not willing to give either of them the satisfaction.

Oh, and did I mention that the Countess of Poo is the one who invited me? Yes, that is her nickname. The Countess of Poo. Real mature, huh? I'm so proud of myself.

I think it was a test to see if I would actually come, so yeah, she is playing this game even more than I am. She has never said as much, but I can tell she is not a fan of mine thanks to the fake pleasantries and forced smiles I have been getting all week. Not going to lie, I'm kind of enjoying that she is threatened by me.

As I stand in front of my mirror with my bikini on, I let out a huge sigh. I bet Candace looks way better in her bikini. She has a perfect stick thin body whereas I definitely do not.

Man, where did all of my confidence go?

"You ready?" She bellows from outside my door, annoying me.

"Yeah, I'll be right out."

"Dylan is outside waiting, so hurry up."

Ugh. Put on a brave face, Miranda. You can get through this. As I think this, I know I'm lying. I can't even make a lie to myself believable anymore. I have really lost my edge.

I reach under my bed for a bottle, a quick chug of wine should help calm my nerves.

The heat from the mineral water that is flowing all over my body melts away my self-esteem issues and distracts me momentarily from the horror of hanging out with Dylan and his girlfriend, transporting me to a place of beauty and serenity. That serenity is ripped away, though, upon Dylan stripping off his shirt and climbing into the spring right in front of me.

Darn him and his perfectly fit body. The sun reflects off the water droplets that have formed on his chest, gleaming slightly as he shifts under its rays. I spot part of the tattoo on his ribcage before he dips into the water and I think for a moment that it might be a sunflower. This would be strange since he downplayed his love of them the other day, so I have to be mistaken.

Luckily, I have sunglasses on so I can admire his body discreetly. Or at least that's what I thought until I notice the death glare from Candace who then scoots even closer to him, running her manicured hand over his chest as she does. Furry settles into my stomach at the sight of the small touch, surprising me with its ferocity as it does.

"How the hell have ya been, May? Haven't seen you in years. You just stopped comin' and Dylan never said why."

"Oh, uh, life just got in the way of me being able to

come back." I avoid looking at Dylan when I say this. "How've you guys been?"

"Good," Jebb says this as he flexes his arms, "just been working in town and on my dad's ranch up north."

"Cool," I say this awkwardly.

"You have gotten really pretty, May." I turn to Diego, noticing for the first time how he has grown into his once lanky, uncoordinated body. With dark bronzed skin and chestnut hair, he has become the definition of tall, dark, and handsome. I do not immediately know what to do with this revelation, but it occurs to me that maybe Diego is the one I should be admiring behind these sunglasses instead of Dylan. However, the image of him chasing me through the sunflowers with a handful of fresh cow manure *screeches* into my mind, quickly putting the brakes on the thought.

"Oh, thanks, Diego. Can you call me Miranda, though? I dropped that nickname a while ago." In my peripheral vision, Dylan subtly twitches, making me regret saying anything.

"Sure thing, Miranda. I didn't even know that was your real name, I always thought it was May." When I do not say anything more, he continues, "We should go out sometime while you're here this summer. I can take you to the drive-in."

"The drive-in's still open? I thought they were going to close it down last year." Dylan asks this as I lean back to admire the clear blue sky—and advert my eyes from his body.

"Yup, it's still open and it's still pretty sweet. I mean, there's not a ton of other things to do but chicks seem to dig it. So, what do ya think? Is it a date? How 'bout next weekend?"

"Sure," I say this without it really registering that I'm being asked on a date by the kid who used to flick his boogers at me. It's hard for me to focus on anything but the nearness of Dylan and his perfect lips.

"Let's double!" Pipes the Countess of Poo.

Great. Just *great*.

Chapter Twenty

Dylan

A double date with May and Diego? What could be worse than that?

Nothing. *Absolutely nothing.*

I would rather eat a mud pie covered in dead bugs than sit in a drive-in theater while May and Diego make out in the back of his stupid beat-up Ford truck.

Why would she even agree to that? Is that the type she is into now? *Dumb*? She used to barely tolerate Diego, how is it that she is agreeing to date him now?

My face is directed at Jebb who is droning on about his new horse, but my eyes are on May. Thank God for sunglasses because I can admire her in secret.

She is wearing a bikini that ties in the middle of her chest. Her chest is new for me. I got the idea that it was a pretty great chest when she wore that fitted t-shirt to dinner, but now, I can see it for what it really is and—*man*—I didn't see it coming. When we were fourteen, I don't even think she wore a bra yet. Now, at twenty, they are spilling out over that too small of a bikini top of hers and it is making me think all sorts of things that I shouldn't.

I assume I'm being inconspicuous, but a glare from Candace tells me that I might have been caught, so I lean back and stare at the sky like May is.

We have been in the hot spring for about an hour when we hear a ringing. It is Candace's phone and while she climbs out of the water to answer, I risk another glance in May's direction only to instantly regret it as she is already looking at me. I shoot my eyes back up to Candace.

"That was my dad. My parents are taking me to dinner

in town tonight to celebrate hitting a hundred thousand followers on Instagram, so I had better get back down the mountain." Candace grabs the pink towel she brought and dries off.

I begin to climb out of the water when Candace puts a hand on my shoulder to stop me, "You don't want me to come?" I ask, secretly hoping she says no. I hate having dinner with her parents, they are usually drunk before the appetizers even come.

"No, that's okay. You and I'll have our own celebration later. Can I get a ride with you guys?" Candace says this as she drops the towel and pulls her sundress over the wet suit, her perfect body on full display as she does, something that Jebb and Diego have definitely noticed.

I'm surprised she would leave knowing that May is here with me. Is this some kind of test? It *has* to be. She has asked me several times this week if there is anything going on with us, so I know she is suspicious. Is she upset because she caught me looking at May? Ugh, now I'm dreading that I might be in for a long night of lecturing.

"Are you sure you don't want me to give you a ride back?"

"I'm sure. Why don't you and Miranda hang out for a bit? I know you're old friends and you probably have all kinds of things to talk about." The attitude she uses to speak is thick with annoyance.

Yup, I'm definitely in trouble.

"It's no problem, man, I'll drop her off on the way down the mountain. We've got to get back anyway," Jebb says as he takes one last gulp of the beer he brought, "it was good seeing you again, Miranda. Later, Dyl."

"Later, Jebb." I say without a hint of interest.

"Yeah, later, guys. Jebb's my ride so I got to go, too."

I can tell Diego wishes he could stay and hang out more with May and it annoys me more than it should. "Thanks for the invite, Dyl, oh, and I'll get your number from Dylan and call you about next weekend, Miranda." Diego says this as he also climbs out of the hot spring and grabs his towel.

"Okay, Diego." She sounds quiet when she says this like she is not really paying attention.

I watch as all three of them make their way to Jebb's truck.

And then there were two.

This is crazy. Like a game of chicken, neither May nor I want to be the first to acknowledge that we want to leave, as that would be an indication that one of us is uncomfortable. *Ugh.* I wish she was not so stubborn. The urge to fill this silence with something finally consumes me.

"You really going on a date with Diego?" *Really?* This is all I can think to ask?

"Sure, he's cute. Why not?"

"He's a doofus." I sound like a jealous fool.

"I know . . . but a girl gets lonely."

"Hm. Lonely enough to go on a date with the kid who used to chase us around with manure?"

"If he's such a loser, why're you still friends with him?"

"There's not a lot of people on this mountain and a guy gets lonely." I throw her words back at her with a snark.

She rolls her eyes before changing the subject, "How's things with Candace here?" Her voice is dripping with mockery.

"Great." I said that with a bit too much gusto. "How has it been living with her?" I can play this game too.

"Honestly?"

"That doesn't sound good."

"She's okay. I mean, she's very pretty, but she's kinda dull." Okay, now she wants to fight.

"Dull? How's she dull?"

"She never really has anything to say, Dylan."

"Oh, and you do?"

"Yeah, I have lots to say."

"Like what?"

"Lots of things."

The silence and awkwardness return like an avalanche, encasing us quickly.

"Man, this is awkward, huh?"

I'm grateful for the honesty, but I'm not sure how to respond. I shrug, "I guess so."

"Are we ever going to be normal around each other?"

"We don't need to be. I mean, it's just for the rest of the summer and then we won't see each other anymore, right?" I think I might have said this too harshly because a flash of pain crosses May's face and I instantly feel like an ass.

"Right . . . I need to get going." She caves and I win. I just wish I felt better about it.

"Fine." I begin to climb out of the water and, yet again, I have a hand on my shoulder stopping me. Only this time, it is May's hand, and the touch burns.

She quickly pulls her hand back—it must have burned her, too. "Don't worry about it. I want to walk."

"Don't be ridiculous. It'll take you an hour to get back, I can drive you."

"No, I want to walk. I don't want to sit with you in your car. It's too awkward."

"You know what, fine, walk then." I stomp out of the hot spring and toward my truck, without turning back.

I was right.

After Candace gets back from dinner with her parents, we get into it. She spends the next couple of hours telling me she knows that May wants me and I need to tell her now if I'm sleeping with her.

I repeat myself, "No, I've told you already a million times, I have not ever, nor will I ever sleep with her."

"I saw the way you two were looking at each other today, I'm not stupid, Dylan."

"I want to be with you, Candace, not May. I swear I want to be with you."

"Then quit looking at her when you're with me!" Candace's arms are in the air as she screams this and I just hope my mother can't hear her. This is embarrassing to say the least.

"Okay! I'm sorry! I won't do it again!" Now I'm the one yelling.

"Oh, so you admit you were looking at her?!"

I rake my hands over my face and let out a frustrated sigh, "What do you want from me?"

"I need some time to think about this, Dylan. I'm going to stay at the house tonight, I don't want to be around you right now."

"Come on, Candace, you don't have to do that."

"You should have thought of that before you ogled that girl."

Candace storms out in a huff, leaving me exhausted. The problem is she's right. Something is going on between May and I, and I can't see to figure out how to stop it.

Chapter Twenty-One

Miranda

Later that night, and one cold shower and cup of tea later, I have finally calmed down. Dylan's painful reminder that he does not want anything to do with me has reopened the wounds that took me the last week to heal.

No matter what I do, he keeps rejecting me. We take one step forward followed by five steps back. Why can't I get it through my head? He does not want anything to do with me other than old acquaintances. *Let it go already.*

I snuggle under the sheets of my bed, the warmth of them briefly warming my nervous heart, when I hear a light tapping at the door.

"Miranda? Can I come in?"

"Uh, sure." *Candace?* REALLY?!

Candace opens the door slowly; her expression is unreadable. The moonlight is streaming in through the window above my bed, casting a slight glow across the hardwood floor.

"Uh, hey, do you need something?"

She comes across the room and sits on the edge of my bed, "Can I ask you something?"

Oh no, this is not good, "Sure, what's up, Candace?"

"Are you into Dylan?"

My mouth drops, as I feign surprise, "What?"

"Miranda, please just answer the question."

"Why do you ask me that?" My hands are shaking now, so I tuck them further under the sheets. This is so uncomfortable.

"I dunno, just a vibe I'm getting. I mean you're so weird around me and you're especially weird with Dylan. I keep seeing you staring at him and stuff. He told me that you two have a history, you were friends or whatever and only kissed once, so I know it's not a big deal, but I just wanted to make sure you weren't into him." I cannot believe he told her we kissed. Exactly which kiss was he referring to?

"Oh, no, Candace, I mean, he's with you and we're just childhood friends."

"That doesn't answer my question."

"Um . . . no, I'm not into him, Candace." What else can I say? *Yes, your boyfriend is making me crazy and he belongs to me, always has.*

"Good. Because I think I'm in love with him and I don't want some random old friend of his getting in the way of our future." I really hate this girl.

"I get it."

"Okay, can we be friends?" She says this with the fake bitterness that only a woman can do.

"Sure." She knows I don't mean it.

As much as I want to hate Candace, though, the fleeting, pained look in her eyes still manages to make me feel like crap, but I can't help but notice that she walks up the stairs to one of the guest rooms. This is the first time since she arrived that she has not stayed at Dylan's. *Interesting.*

Even with this information floating around in my head, I know that I have to move past this, I do not want to come between them, I do not want to be that girl in their story, no matter how much I am starting to realize that I want him.

The next few days are relatively normal other than my internal voice screaming at me every second of every hour.

The girl in my head is a wreck. She thinks about that kiss one second, then feels guilty and stupid about it the next. She repeatedly yells at me that I'm a horrible and selfish person. She is incredibly annoying and I have no idea how to make her shut up. The only solution I can come up with—go to the drive-in with Diego.

Even though he has grown into his once awkward body, he is still Diego and he will never hold a candle to Dylan and I know it. I have no real interest in him, but I need to show both Dylan and Candace that I'm not trying to sabotage their relationship, so I forge ahead with Diego. When he calls, I answer, he tells me jokes and I giggle, all the while I'm just holding my breath until this summer is over.

It's Saturday night and the drive-in theatre is a blast from a different time. The large screen has cracks running through it, but no one seems to mind. The pickup trucks are lined up—couples are packed into the backs with their blankets and beer ready to watch whatever low budget feature is playing this week.

Diego places a big blanket and picnic basket in the bed of his Ford and I have to say it is quite adorable. Inside the basket are two ham and cheese sandwiches, a bundle of roses, and a bottle of wine with two glasses. I'm too embarrassed to admit to him that I have a bottle of wine in my backpack already. I figured I was going to need it to get through this night.

We crawl on top of the blankets and prop ourselves up on the pillows Diego brought from his bedroom, the picnic basket between our legs.

"This is amazing, Diego, and so sweet of you."

"I'm glad you like it."

"I love it. I had no idea you were this romantic."

"I'm full of surprises, Miranda." He smiles at me and

his crooked bottom tooth gleams from the light coming from the big screen. Some women out there would probably find it an endearing feature, I on the other hand, do not.

"Hey, guys!" The Countess of Poo yells out from Dylan's Chevy. He pulls up—of course—right beside us because my life has become comically ridiculous. Dylan has one hand draped over the wheel while Candace is leaned over him to yell at us through his open window. He is wearing his lucky green hat that he always wore as a kid. It is beat up pretty bad, but that somehow only adds to its charm. To my surprise, he turns and makes direct eye contact with me. This is the first time he has done this since tent-gate. I'm too busy looking at his lips and thinking of what they felt like on mine to hear Diego say my name.

"Miranda? Did you hear me?"

"Uh, yeah. Sorry, I was just distracted I think. . . ." *Crap*, I had just begun to think I would be able to forget about that kiss and here he is, forcing me right back to it. "What's up?"

"I was just asking if you'd like to have some wine?" YES.

"Oh, sure. Thank you." As Diego pours, I turn back to face Dylan.

"Hey, you two. Glad you could make it." NOT.

"Is that a picnic basket?" Dylan asks while climbing up into the bed of his truck, a single blanket and nothing else in hand.

"Sure is, man, you got to do what you can, you know?" Diego belts this out over the top of my head, he is clearly impressed with himself.

"Man, I missed the mark then tonight."

"Yeah, you did." Candace scrunched face clearly demonstrating her dissatisfaction. The interaction delights me to the core.

I'm trying to focus on the movie and on being a good date to Diego but it is taking every ounce of strength I have. I never once turn my head in Candace and Dylan's direction, the fear that I will see them kissing has me petrified. Luckily, smooching sounds are never heard, but the movie is loud enough that I'm not sure I would. The thought of their lips touching hurts so bad I think it might kill me.

Diego wraps his arm around my shoulder, and I know he wants to kiss me, but I cannot bring myself to do it. In an odd way, it feels wrong with Dylan so close. I might kiss him later when he is dropping me off at home and I know Dylan cannot see.

"I need some snacks; I'll be right back. Want anything?"

"Some M&Ms would be great."

"Hey, either of you want some candy or something?" Dylan interrupts us and is standing at the end of Diego's truck bed. His fitted white t-shirt and green hat are in full view, disturbing me on every level.

"Yeah, I was just going to go grab some popcorn and May wants M&Ms."

"She goes by Miranda now." Did I hear annoyance in Dylan's voice?

"Oh, sure, sorry, Miranda. I keep forgetting." I smile at Diego to let him know it's okay.

"Miranda, come with." Why does he want me to come with him? Like the true pathetic person that I am, I jump at the chance to be near him. I also notice, annoyingly, the twinge in my stomach every time I hear Dylan call me Miranda. It sounds so forced and out of place. I hate it. I made such an ordeal about not being called May, though, that I can't stop him now. *Ugh.*

"I'll be right back, Diego," I say this quickly before Diego can stop me.

"Oh, okay." Diego slumps back down, looking defeated.

Dylan offers his hand so that I can get down from the truck and I take it, only to immediately regret it. Even the slightest touch cascades throughout my body like a ripple. I think he feels it, too, because he lets go briskly.

Out of earshot of Diego, Dylan takes the chance to say his peace. "I just wanted to check in with you and see how you're doing . . . I mean, I haven't had a chance to check in with you since Candace got here and the other day at the hot springs didn't seem like the right time but I've been a bit worried about you."

It takes me a second to remember the drunken panic attack on the porch from a couple of weeks ago. "Oh, no problem. You don't need to worry about me, or check in on me. I'm fine, Dylan. I was just having a weird day. No biggie. Thanks, though." I ignore how happy it makes my heart that Dylan is worried about me.

"Good. I'm glad. You can always talk to me if you need to ya' know?"

"I can?"

"Yes, I know things are awkward, but if you ever needed me, really needed me, I'm here." I nod and I smile because deep down, I know he means it.

"Oh, and thanks for not saying anything to Candace about the tent thing. And I'm sorry I was kind of a dick at the hot spring. It wasn't necessary." Wow, he is apologizing and thanking me? Maybe our friendship has a chance after all.

"No problem. I've resigned myself to the fact that

things will always be weird between us. You know I would never rat you out about the tent thing, right? Even though we are weird now, I wouldn't do that. You could call me tomorrow and need help burying a body and I would be all over it. Plus, I don't want to cause you two problems. She's crazy over you. She told me so the other night."

"Yeah, and I her." The knife in my heart turns slightly, increasing the sharp pain in my chest. So, does that mean he loves her? "What did she say to you?"

"Just that she wanted to make sure there was nothing going on between us. I assured her that there wasn't." I smile up at him, but he doesn't smile back.

"I didn't know she did that. That must have been weird for you."

I shrug, "I guess it was a bit, but I don't want to cause you problems." It's true. I don't. Do I want the Countess of Poo to fall into a vat of boiling oil? Yes. Do I want to cause Dylan problems? No.

Dylan nods before continuing, "So, how are things with Diego? He has really gone above and beyond for this date." I cannot help but think this is a loaded question, like he is hoping I say it is going horribly and I hate Diego, but I'm desperate for him to think that I'm not hung up on him. So, I lie. Again.

"Things are good. He has called me a couple of times and, I have to say, he's super sweet. He's not at all like I remember." I build him up, made brave by the hurt I feel for Dylan's potential love for Candace.

"That was a long time ago, May, we've all changed a lot since then." No kidding. I notice he calls me May and since my heart surges with warmth, I don't correct him.

We arrive at the concession stand and I reach for M&Ms while he grabs a cookies-and-cream candy bar.

"I can't believe that you still like that. That's the

grossest candy bar on the planet!"

"You just have no taste buds and can't appreciate its deliciousness." He says this with a toothy grin, then puts the wrapped candy bar into his mouth for a half-hearted bite.

I scrunch my face, "EW, Dylan, you have no idea whose hands have touched that wrapper!" He tries to appear outraged but his laughter tells me otherwise.

I have always loved Dylan's laugh, and it is just the same as it was when were kids: loud and filled with snorts. While some might find it annoying, it is music to my ears and as the sound fills the night sky, my attraction to him is becoming harder and harder to ignore.

As we near the trucks with our dates anxiously waiting, Dylan puts his hand on my elbow to get my attention. "Hey, Miranda? I would help you bury a body, too, you know."

It doesn't sound like a romantic sentence, but it is in fact the most romantic thing anyone has ever said to me.

Chapter Twenty-Two

Dylan

Despite the strangeness of the situation, I have a good time at the drive-in.

The drive back to the ranch was not so great, however, as the time is spent with Candace grilling me about why I wanted to take May to the concession stand and not her. I knew it was a risky move when I did it, but I did it on an impulse. When I got up to get snacks, I chanced a glance to May and Diego and saw how close Diego was leaning into her. For a split second, panic shot through me that he was going to kiss her. Before I could think about what I was doing, I jumped in and asked her to come with me. My heart did summersaults when she eagerly accepted the invite. I took the opportunity to talk with her and check in and try to clear the air. I'm proud for where we ended it—as friends. However, two days later I'm still thinking about her and that kiss all the time, and so the victory is short lived. I have since spent an abundant amount of mental energy trying to push down the growing issue I have with May.

Yes, that is what I am calling it now. The 'issue.'

To resolve the 'issue', I choose a healthy option. Ignoring it and shoving any feelings other than mild annoyance I have towards her into the depths of brain, hoping it will get lost in there, never to be heard from again. Like I said, *healthy.*

I wish I could say things were back on track with Candace, but saying things are tense between us would be putting it mildly. I'm acutely aware that Candace and I did not make out at the drive-in. I am also aware that kissing is the entire point of taking a girl to the drive-in. There was a moment when she leaned in and I could tell that she wanted to, so I shoved candy into my mouth so she couldn't. She glanced at me with a suspicious scowl but I pretended not to notice. Am I interested in diving into the reasons I avoided making out with my super-hot girlfriend at the movies? No. Absolutely not.

To make matters worse, Candace and I have not had sex since the fight after the day at the hot spring. She has also not stayed at my house, either. I suspect she wants me to beg her to stay with me, but I cannot bring myself to do it. If I'm completely honest with myself, in a way, I feel like I am being unfaithful to May. I know. It is *absurd*. I have added it to a growing list of things that I'm ignoring and push it with the rest of them into the deepest recesses of my brain.

As if things could not get any worse for me this summer, I have developed other concerns. I have not told anyone yet—not even my grandfather—but I'm worried about my mom. A couple of days ago she was in her bathroom throwing up and when I asked her if she was okay, she was mortified I heard her get sick and refused to answer my question with any detail. After this happened, I started to notice other little things, like she has lost even more weight, and looks pale all the time.

It is Wednesday morning and the time in the morning when my mom is usually making Rusty breakfast. Instead of finding her with Rusty, she is asleep on the couch. This is highly unusual. My entire life, my mom as always been a morning person, I have never, not one time in my twenty-one years, seen her take a single nap.

I nervously tug on her leg, "Mom? Why're you sleeping? Are you feelin' okay?"

She startles a bit but leaps off the couch as soon as she realizes what's going on. "Oh, I'm sorry, Dylan, I'm just fighting a cold. Don't worry about it." She folds the blanket haphazardly. "I need to get Rusty his breakfast.

Poor guy's probably pretty confused right now."

"Okay, do you need help? I can do it."

"No, Dyl, I always get his breakfast. I can do it." She bites this out, clearly annoyed.

"Fine, let me know if you need anything."

"I will dear. Thanks for checking in on me. So, how have things been between you and May?"

"Really, Mom? Why do you keep asking me that?"

"I'm just curious. I know you missed her when she stopped coming here."

"Please, that was years ago, I don't want to talk about it."

"Okay, but just one last thing and I will drop it. Don't hold on to the pain from the past, Dylan. It's a waste of time and energy. Forgive her."

"Can we drop it?"

"Yes, of course."

I love my mother a great deal. She has always been a badass. She raised me as both mother and father after I lost my dad and she never complained once. She works hard on the ranch, better than any ranch hand we have ever had, and she is smart and loving. However, her recent obsession about all things between May and me has become crazy annoying. I cut her some slack, though, because I'm worried about her.

It has been two days and my worries for my mom's health only increase as she seems more tired than ever. I catch her sleeping now at all times of the day and in random places around the house and barn. One day, she was sound asleep next to Sally in her stable and when I woke her up, she denies she was even asleep. She is obviously trying to keep something from me, and my gut tells me it's not good. I try to distract myself from it by spending as much time with Candace as possible, but it's hard. She is suspicious of everything I do now, and we rarely have any fun together anymore, as our conversations ultimately end up about May and our relationship. It is exhausting. Plus, she is not exactly the best at knowing when something is upsetting me, and I'm starting to think that she really does not know me at all.

What surprises me—although maybe it shouldn't—is that May notices. One evening, as I sat on her front porch waiting for Candace to finish getting ready for our date, May comes outside to say hello. We are both really trying to be friendly towards each other ever since my peacemaking at the drive-in, so she goes out of her way to come outside and say hello each time I come to pick up Candace, and I do the same anytime I see her. On this particular evening, I had just spent dinner with Mom and noticed she didn't touch her food so my anxiety was high, and it must have been noticeable—at least it was to May.

"Is everything okay with you, Dylan? I know I don't know you that well anymore, but you've seemed a bit off lately."

"Oh, uh, yup. I'm totally fine. It's nothing."

May and I used to know everything about each other. I could tell from a distance if something was wrong even if she never said anything. I knew every time she was annoyed with me or upset about something. I could tell if she needed a hug or just wanted to hang out. I just understood her. I never put much thought into if she could read me the same way or not. I was always too focused on trying to make sure she was happy to notice. However, when she asked me if I was okay, it shook me. Maybe she has always been able to read me, too, and maybe, that connection was not completely lost.

It is hot out. Too hot. The oppression from the rays of the sun rage war on my skin even as I wade into the cool water of the pond. I climb out of the water and trek carefully over to the big pine tree, careful not to cut my bare feet on the twigs or rocks littering the ground.

Candace is sitting on the edge of the pond with water just up to her knees. This is the farthest she has gotten in, while May and Diego are diving in and competing to see who can swim the fastest. I have learned in the time Candace has been here, just how *not* into the outdoors she is. She likes to do some things, like hiking short distances and riding horses, but only for the purposes of an image to put on her social media page. She never actually seems to touch the dirt or grass or trees. It is as though she is more interested in looking at nature then interacting with it.

May is different. Even when we were kids, she was never afraid to get dirty. She wanted her hands on every piece of earth she could touch. She loves it, breathes it, and flourishes in it. Even though she has not been here in years, she has leaped headfirst right back into it.

I try not to compare them—May and Candace—but it's hard not to. They are just so *different* from each other. I have tried to think of anything they have in common but came up short. Diego pointed it out to me earlier today while we waited for the girls to get their swimsuits on.

"Candace is cool."

"Uh. Yeah. She is."

"She's not really the type that I thought you would date though."

"What do you mean?" May's porch swing creaks as I rock it back and forth while Diego leans against the front door.

"I don't know. She's just not outdoorsy, I guess. I always thought you would end up with Miranda, or someone like her."

"Well, I like Candace."

"I get it, she's super-hot. Don't take offense man, just an observation."

I do take offense, though, and the comment has been bothering me all day. In fact, everything about him is bothering me. He has been around a lot lately and while he is one of my oldest friends and I normally like to hang out with him, I cannot ignore how his growing relationship with May is disturbing the cells in body.

As I watch the sun reflect off their wet shoulders; their eyes shine bright and wide; their laughter echoing against the trees, I cannot help but be transported to when we were kids, back at this very pond.

"Dylan...DYLAN!"

"Oh my god, May, what?!" This is the hundredth question she has asked me today but all I want to do is swim.

"Why do think the sky is blue?" May is always doing this, asking me questions I don't know the answer to. I try to come up with something that sounds smart, though.

"Hmm . . . I think it has to do with the molecules that are in the sky. They look blue to us." My body is cool in the water, but my arms are warm because I have them stretched out on the bank before me. May is to the right of me laying in the dirt along the edge. She was tired of swimming and had climbed out so that she could lay out and capture the sun's rays.

"Oh." May scrunches her face as she considers my hypothesis. "I think it's the reflection of the oceans."

"That could be, makes sense to me."

May flips over on her side, using one arm to prop her head up. Her long hair falls to the side, some of it laying in the dirt. I would tell her, but she does not mind it when her hair is dirty. The sun is bright around us, blowing slightly, cooling the water droplets on our skin.

"Dylan and May kissing in a tree," Diego sings as he gets out of the water and runs over to us with Jebb right behind him laughing.

"Shut up, Diego, we are not." May's face scrunches with disgust as she says this. My heart hurts a little when she does.

Diego starts making kissing noises and my face turns hot from embarrassment, "She said shut up!"

I jump up at the same time Diego does and just like that we are off running—me close behind him and May close behind me.

"Wait for me!"

"You can't catch us, you're just a girl!" Jebb bellows out as he races past May and tries to catch me.

I turn back and see May running as fast as she can, and I hold out my hand to her. She takes it and I pull her along close behind the others.

"Why are you being weird?" The sound of Candace's voice jolts me back to the present.

"Am I?"

"Yes, Dylan. You've been acting weird all day."

"Oh, I'm sorry. I guess I have a lot on my mind."

"Is this about them?" Candace asks with her arms crossed as she nods her head in Diego and May's direction.

"No, of course not. I've told you that. I don't want to keep talking about it." Please, not this conversation again.

"Then what is it?"

"I was thinking about my mom. . . she's been sick

lately."

"Oh, well, I'm sure she'll be fine. Now get back to focusing on me. Here, take a few pics of me for Insta while we're here."

"Okay, sure." I grab her phone and snap some pictures of the beautiful girl before me, only to look over her shoulder, watching May and Diego swimming in the background.

Chapter Twenty-Three

Miranda

Something is wrong.

Dylan has been weird and depressed lately and it has made my already stressed self so much more stressed that I barely know what to do with myself. I want to hug and talk to him, but I can't, and it is making me crazy not knowing what it is that is upsetting him. The narcissist in me believes that it is about Diego. I have embraced this 'relationship' with Diego for a couple of reasons; one is that I can use him to convince Candace that I am not crazy in love with her man, the other, more honest reason, is to make Dylan jealous. I doubt he has even a shred of the jealous rage I do, but the thought still comforts me.

There is a downside to this set up with Diego and it's a big one. To me its fake, to him, its real and he wants to move forward. I won't be able to keep up this charade much longer if I don't kiss him soon. I'm sure he has started to wonder if I'm a prude, a virgin or maybe a lesbian. I had considered kissing him after the drive-in when he dropped me off at my front porch, but when he leaned forward, Dylan's face flashed through my head. So, instead, I ran inside, claiming a sudden headache. At the pond yesterday, he tried again by flirting all day, and he even leaned in twice and got within an inch of my mouth before I dodged him both times.

Time is running out though and I know it. The frustrating thing is that it's not fair to him. I'm single and, technically, I should *want* to kiss him. He is cute, and funny, sweet, and nothing at all like he once was. Plus, he is fit and tall and just the type of guy I would normally be all over.

The guilt over how I'm treating Diego creates an uncomfortably heavy sensation in my chest but I brush it aside, not wanting to dwell on it. I'll let him down soon enough, but I need this to last as long as possible, or at least until this retched summer ends and I can get out of here.

As I finish the salad I made for lunch on this warm, perfect day, my mind drifts back to Dylan. He came to pick up Candace this morning to take her to town to do some shopping and I wonder if they are having a good time, although they did not seem to the other day at the pond. Dylan was not himself as he swam quietly in the water, barely spoke to her, or anyone, and not a single smile graced his handsome face. This is odd because swimming at this pond has always been one of his favorite things to do. Maybe my fake relationship is not the only thing that is bothering him and something is *really* wrong. The jealous part of me hopes it has to do with his relationship with Candace.

This is the problem with us. I know him too well. I have always been able to sense when something is off with him.

Once when we were twelve, Dylan's horse Peter died. He kept saying that it was okay, and he was fine with it and to let it go but I could just tell he was devastated. He was quiet and did not seem to enjoy doing anything and no matter what I did, I couldn't get that dimple of his to pop.

To cheer him up, I had climbed onto the roof of his house and snuck in a letter and a drawing I did of Peter onto the desk underneath his window while he slept. I did not disturb him that night, I wanted him to wake up to the drawing and be surprised. He loved my drawings and was always asking me to draw him stuff, so I knew he would like it.

The letter I wrote told him that Peter loved him and would miss him. The drawing showed Peter with wings. The next morning when I woke up, I looked out my window and there he was, waiting for me under the pine tree, so I knew it worked and he was feeling better. When I walked outside to meet him, he hugged me. He never said anything—just wrapped his arms around me tightly in the biggest bear hug possible.

Now, after seeing him at the pond, the desire to cheer him up is just as strong as it was back then. Maybe another drawing will do the trick—I'm a much better artist than I was when I was twelve, so I could really do something decent for him. I dig out my old colored pencils along with a small canvas from the storage closet under the stairs and settle back at the dining room table.

The idea of what to draw comes to me immediately and after about an hour, a picture of the ranch with his house, mom, and sheepdog Rusty in the center with the mountains in the background emerges. I stand up and step back to look at it from a distance and I have to say, it's not half bad. *How am I going to get it to him without Candace knowing?* I'm not delusional enough to think that she would be fine with me giving him a gift of any kind, especially a handmade one. I consider climbing on his roof after dark, but the image of me clambering around and humiliating myself like the last time dashes away that idea.

We have plans to do some horseback riding up the west trail this afternoon, so maybe I will get a chance to sneak the gift to him then.

My phone pings and I know it is Diego without looking, telling me he is outside, so I put the drawing for Dylan and a bottle of sweet red wine into my backpack and head out. That reminds me that I need to restock the cellar soon. Luckily, my drinking went unnoticed when my mom was here with the tenants. It was only because I had replaced most of the bottles already and the ones I hadn't I left on the shelf hoping she would not notice they were empty. She never even thought to pick any of them up. She just counted to make sure they were all there and left it at that.

As soon as the screen door slams behind me, Candace and Dylan come into view. They toss their backpacks into the back of Diego's truck, then Dylan grabs shopping bags from his truck and passes me with a brief smile on his way to drop them off inside the house. My heart aches from the urge to reach out and touch him. I reach the passenger side door, mumbling hello to Candace to which she mumbles hello back. It makes sense that we would all ride over together, but my jealous heart fractures when I turn and watch Dylan carefully lift Candace into the bed of the truck, who giggles when he pats her behind. I try and recover quickly as I climb into the passenger side, shutting the door behind me.

"Hey, beautiful, how're you?" Diego really is sweet. Maybe I will give him a real chance.

"Hey, Diego. I'm good. I'm ready to do some riding."

"Alrighty, let's go!" With a quick glance in the side mirror, I spot Dylan's dimple with his smile directed at Candace and I die just a little more inside.

My hand rubs over my backpack, comforted with the knowledge of what's in it.

The heat waves are breaking through the clouds and slapping my shoulders with their aggression.

Needing to cool off, I take a quick break and jump off Sally, handing her reigns over to Diego. Dylan and

Candace are somewhere behind us, probably taking photos of Candace.

"Hey, take her for a second. I'm going to walk into the trees and take a quick break."

"Cool, do you want me to come with?"

"No, it's fine."

"Oh, have to pee?"

"Uh. Yeah."

"Gotcha. I'll be waiting."

I do not have to pee, but I do need a moment to myself, so I walk briskly down towards the small creek that runs through both the Ryder's and my parents' properties. It is shrouded in trees and the perfect spot to cool off in private. The creek is a small, muddy place but it has the rope swing that Dylan and I used to spend hours on and the same one that I dropped once when Dylan got hurt. The rope was later tied tight by Mrs. Ryder so that we wouldn't have to rely on one of us holding it to use it.

I inch my way down the narrow path until I get to the spot where I can put my feet in the shaded mountain water. Barefoot and standing on pebbles in the shallow creek, I pull out that bottle of wine from my backpack. After Dylan has caught me a couple of times, I know I need to keep my drinking on the down low from him, so I look around me before opening it. I don't want him thinking I have some kind of problem—*because I don't.*

Right now, the sweet wine sounds like a perfect accompaniment to my warm skin and cool feet. I set the bottle down beside my bag when something dark catches my eye. I'm so lost in thought that I do not immediately notice the figure on the opposite side of the water, walking towards me.

The figure startles me for a moment with concerns of it being a wild animal but my fear levels off as I recognize it as Dylan.

"Sorry, didn't mean to scare you." *Damn, where did he come from?*

I clutch my chest, "Oh, uh, no it's okay. I just didn't expect you. What're you doing out here?"

"It's peaceful down here by this creek. I like the sound of the water. It calms me down. Plus, it got too hot riding and I needed to pee."

"Where's Candace?"

"She's taking a few selfies with the horses." Of course, she is.

"Oh. Why do you need to calm down, anyway?"

"Oh, just got a lot on my mind. What about you? What're you doin' down here?"

"I just needed some shade."

"Hm . . . is that wine?" He is close enough now that I can't deny it.

"Oh, yeah. I forgot it was in my backpack, I was considering taking a drink of it." I say this in my best nonchalant tone, but I can tell by the way he is chewing his lip that he is not buying my act.

"You seem to really like wine." The statement catches me off guard and it takes me a moment before it registers what he is trying to insinuate. I brush it aside quickly.

"Sure, yeah. I do. I guess. What's wrong with liking wine?"

"I don't know. Nothing, I guess. It just seems like you drink it at weird times."

"Don't be so judgmental, Dylan. I'm a young women stuck on a mountain with not much else to do."

"Okay, fair enough."

My nerves get the best of me so I reach for the bottle and take a big gulp. He has already seen it; I might as well enjoy a drink.

"I've been worried about my mom lately." *Awesome,* a subject change. This I can handle.

"What do you mean?" A bit of red courage dribbles down my chin and I wipe it off quickly.

"She seems sick, but it's like she doesn't want to tell me about it."

"She does seem like she's lost weight, but I haven't seen her in so long I wasn't sure."

"It's not just her weight, it's that she sleeps a lot and doesn't eat and I've even caught her puking a couple of times."

"Oh no, that's not good. You better go in there and insist she explains what's going on." So, *this* is what's been bothering him.

Dylan lifts the corner of his mouth in an almost smile before reaching out for the bottle. I stretch over the small creek to hand it to him. He wraps his hand around it, careful not to touch me, and takes a large drink. I try not to notice his Adam's apple as he swallows.

"This is not good."

I chuckle, "No, it's not the best."

"Why're you drinking it then?"

I shrug and pick up a pebble by my feet, rolling it around in my hand, admiring its smooth surface. We are back on this topic and I don't want to be.

"Is there something going on that you're not telling me?" I scrunch my face at him in mock horror but he calls me out on it. "Come on, I've caught you drinking this stuff on a couple of occasions now. And at weird times. Is this a problem for you? Drinking?"

"Depends on who you ask."

"I'm asking you."

"Drop it, Dylan. It's none of your business." This comes out way harsher than I intend, but I do not need him questioning my drinking, I have it under control.

As he hands me back the bottle, my hand grazes his, causing a current to shoot down to the tips of my toes.

It's as though I have been struck by a stun gun and now my nerve endings are ablaze.

I look up into his face and realize he felt it too, thanks to the tightening of his jawline as he looms over me.

"I made you something." The words fumble out of my mouth nervously.

"You made me something?" Dylan's eyes go wide with surprise.

"Yeah, you have seemed down lately so I thought I would try to cheer you up." I reach into the backpack and pull out the drawing. "I was trying to figure out how to get it to you."

"Did you draw this?"

"Yes," I shrug.

"Wow, thanks, Miranda. It's awesome, I love it."

"I didn't want Candace to see it because I don't think she would like the idea of me giving you a gift. You might want to lie and say it came from someone else. Or you bought it or something."

"I'm not going to lie about it, May. Not to anyone." The sternness in his voice stirs my insides, tightening in my chest. He likes it.

"Thanks for noticing. And caring. I guess we really are friends again, huh?" Dylan smiles wide, dimple twinkling. My heart flutters.

"Yeah. Sure. Friends." I smile too.

What *was* that? Why is it that my heart beats wildly at the sight of him? Why is it that I am lying in my bed hours later thinking about that smile?

My head is reeling as I hide under the comforter of my bed.

I slip my hand out from under the cover to grab the wine bottle. I gulp down another drink hoping it will make these strange feelings go away. Surely, it's not love. Surely, I do not *love* him.

As I rip the covers off over my head, I say in a forceful voice, "It was nothing. Love is not real. You know this, Miranda. Get it together."

Chapter Twenty-Four

Dylan

I trace the drawing May gave me with careful and slow precision as though the image is a living breathing thing and I must be careful not to hurt it. The smooth feel of the colored pencil spreads a warmth from my fingertips up my forearm.

The sun is blazing through my bedroom window while the curtains flutter in the warm breeze. The room is alive with light and shadows. My bare feet scrape along the wood floor as I cross the room to tuck the drawing into an old wooden picture frame that I found in the attic. I slip it over the nail in my wall that used to hang my green baseball cap. I would much rather have this drawing staring down at me than that old hat, even if it is my favorite. I do not have much in the way of decoration in this room, I guess I'm a typical guy in that way. A simple gray comforter, a dresser, my baseball cap, and a few pairs of shoes and boots are about it.

I was not going to hang it up, but something about the way she looked at me when she handed it to made me want to. It was a bashful look and I could tell she was worried I wouldn't like it. I do, though, more than I should. It reminds me of the picture she drew of my horse Peter that died when I was twelve. I was devastated about losing him and so May drew me a picture of him with wings to cheer me up. With the memory playing in my head, I walk over to my bed and drop down on the floor beside it, lifting the blankets so that I can see underneath the bed frame. Lying amongst a few pairs of socks and fluffs of sheepdog fur, is that very drawing. I slide my hand under the bed and grip the paper, not wanting to damage it any more than it already is, and pull it out. It still looks the same as I remember it, just dustier now. I remember wanting to throw it away after she stopped talking to me, along with any other item that reminded me of her, but I couldn't bring myself to do it.

I had a few things of hers, a pair of shoes, the toothbrush she would use when she stayed over on Tuesday nights, and a dozen drawings she made over the years. They were mostly of the sunflowers. While everything else was thrown out, I could not bring myself to get rid of this specific drawing, or one of the sunflowers she drew. My favorite one. That one is hidden in my desk. I stand up and go to my desk, wanting to find it now. I rummage around the drawer until I spot it, folded in half. On first glance, it does not seem like much but as I unfold it and run my palm over the old drawing to get the dust off of it, my heart tightens. This flower means more to me than anyone knows. More than I want to think about. I take this drawing and walk back over to the one she gave me yesterday. I slide the small sunflower into the inside of the frame surrounding the new one and stare at them side by side. It was like the old May was back yesterday and it broke my heart all over again. She was sweet and thoughtful and radiating. My stomach lurches into my throat when the image of Diego and May holding hands as they rode the horses back to the ranch flashes in my head. My chest starts to heave as I see the image of him leaning in and giving her a peck on the cheek.

Are they sleeping together? The thought burns across the ridges of my brain. I have no right to feel this way. I have no right to even care. May is not mine. She can sleep with whomever she wants. Regardless of the fact that I know this, it does not stop my head from burning like it is on fire. *Is he going to celebrate her birthday with her?*

Today is June twenty-sixth and May's birthday is coming up very soon. July second to be exact. Over the years, I would try to keep myself busy on her birthdays. After losing her, July second went from being my favorite day of the year, to being the worst. The memory of the last birthday of hers we spent together always haunts me in the weeks leading up to it.

While I stare at the drawings, the memory of that very birthday comes to life in my mind.

"What do you want to do for your birthday this year?"
"Same thing as always. Hang out with you and go for a ride on Sally."
"Do you want me to invite anyone? Like Diego or Jebb?"
"Sure. As long as I can eat chocolate cake with chocolate frosting and your mom makes one of her famous bonfires, then I'll be happy."
"Done and done." May's smile stretches wide, she always gets so excited for her birthday and it's infectious. I love the way it lights up her face.
When the day arrives, we go through it the same as always. I wait for her to wake up in the morning by sitting under the pine outside her window. She comes running out with shorts and a tank top on and jumps into my arms.
"Happy birthday!"
"Thanks, Dyl! Are you excited for today?"
"Of course, let's go."
We spend the first part of the day riding my horses around the ranch while her parents and my mom prepare lunch and bake the cake. Diego and Jebb arrive at one and we all sit around and eat, laughing and enjoying the warm sun.
By evening, my mom has built the biggest bonfire ever.

The grown-ups have a couple of drinks and Diego and Jebb head home leaving May and I mostly to ourselves.

"How was it today?"

"Perfect, as always."

I smile so big it hurts. "I'm glad." We are sitting on a blanket by the bonfire, full to the brim with cake and s'mores. I cross my legs so that my knee is touching hers and put my hands in my lap. Then something happens that I never see coming. May puts her hand on top of mine, turning it over in hers. Then she laces her fingers through my fingers. We have never held hands before and suddenly my chest constricts. I think it's happiness that causes it.

"Dyl?"

"Yeah?"

"I made you something."

"It's your birthday, May, you're the one who should be getting gifts, not me."

"I know, but I don't care."

She pulls a small piece of paper out of her back pocket and hands it to my free hand. It's a colored pencil drawing of a sunflower and it has yellow spots all around it.

"What are those?"

"It's the sunlight. Do you like it?"

May is always drawing sunflowers, but this one has to be my favorite because of the way she drew the sunlight.

"Yes. It's beautiful. I'll keep it forever." She smiles and squeezes my hand again.

I stare into the orange and yellows of the bonfire, while my heart swells. Maybe she does like me as more than a friend. Maybe, just maybe, I'm the luckiest person alive.

Little did I know that I was far from lucky and that

this would be one of the last good memories I have with May. Little did I know that my heart was about to break and nothing would ever be the same.

I stare at the drawings, suddenly wishing she had never given either of them to me. I want the pain to go away and while I would love nothing more than for us to pick up where we left off—my heart won't allow it.

Chapter Twenty-Five

Miranda

I have not been myself lately.

I know this because I'm drinking more and more and leaving my room less and less.

The urge to retreat within myself is overwhelming and powerful. This happens every year around my birthday. I shut down.

To make this birthday even worse than normal, it has become impossible to deny what is right in front of me: I am in love with Dylan Ryder.

I *really* do not want to feel what I do for Dylan because feelings lie. Love is an illusion brought on by evolution to encourage us to procreate. Nothing about it is special, or magical, or cosmic, or related to some deeper level, that has to do with souls and fate or any of that garbage.

No, we are simply being tricked into believing that one person is more special than another, all for the purposes of keeping our genes going for another generation.

The problem is that while I know this, I still cannot help but notice the way my stomach flutters and my pulse increases whenever I hear his voice, see that dimple, or get lost in those eyes of his. It is as though my brain and my body are on two separate wavelengths.

What does it mean and how do I get over it? Well, this red liquid cooling my lips and warming my insides certainly seems to be a good place to start.

It has been three days and I'm now forced to leave the safety of my room and be productive because the Winters are worried about me, so much so that they contacted my mother to tell her that I forgot to wash and replace their sheets and towels. They are very caring people.

After a long and tedious phone call with my mother, where she lectured me for thirty minutes about the importance of being a good host, I slide out from under the covers and press my feet onto the cool surface of the wood floor. It is still early; the sun is only just beginning to rise and there is a wash of muted orange spread out over the landscape outside my window.

The abrupt and unexpected movement of my body from the bed to the floor causes a dull ache in my wine-hazy head. After only having wine and zero food for three days, I should not be surprised by how crappy I feel. I throw on some jeans and a t-shirt and do not bother to apply any makeup or even brush my hair as I stumble out of my bedroom into the hallway towards the kitchen.

A quick patter of delicate footsteps descends the stairs before I have the chance to run back to my room and, suddenly, I'm face to face with Candace. Because, *of course*, I am.

"Uh, wow, Miranda. You really look . . . interesting."

"Thanks, it's a new look I'm trying out. The *'I don't give a crap'* look." I bark this lovely statement at her with a force that is both delicate and lady-like.

"Geesh, Miranda, I don't know why I ever worried about you with Dylan. He'd have to be desperate." She says this in a sardonic manner as she sashays away from me and my already unpleasant mood is now filled with pure unadulterated rage.

A cold shower and numerous cups of coffee later and I'm finally starting to feel normal again. I replace the precious towels and sheets for the Winters and in a not-so-subtle attempt to get back at Candace, I *accidently* put her tablet through the washing machine. It is the same one she spends hours editing photos of herself on.

Oops.

Chapter Twenty-Six

Dylan

Candace is screaming.

Her face is tight and skewed as she waves her arms frantically around and paces the floor of my bedroom.

"Can you believe that?! She actually said it was an accident. How could it be an accident? My tablet was on the kitchen table when I left and somehow it ends up in the washing machine? She's going to pay for this. I'm going to leave the worst review of that dumpy house the second I leave this place. I'll destroy any chance they have of ever renting that place out again!"

I have no idea how to respond. I have no idea if May did it on purpose or not and I am not sure what Candace expects from me, so I sit quietly and listen.

While she yells, my mom walks by the open door and glances in, raising her eyebrows before scuttling away. This is the fastest I have seen her move this entire summer.

"Why would she do it on purpose?" This is apparently not the right question to ask because Candace turns to me with wild eyes.

"Because she's desperate and jealous. She wants you and can't have you. Plus, I'm just all around better than her, Dylan. That's why. Jealously. A tale as old as time."

While Candace rants, my phone buzzes in my pocket. She is too hysterical to notice so I pull my phone out and check it. To my surprise, it is a message from Diego.

Hey Dyl, sorry to bug you. I'm sure I'm just being ghosted but I wanted to check. Is Miranda okay? She hasn't responded to me in days and I thought things were cool. Was just kind of worried about her. If you could let me know that she's okay, that would be great. Thanks man.

First the tablet and now she is not speaking to Diego anymore? Something is not right.

Chapter Twenty-Seven

Miranda

I'm back in my safe space. My bed.

After a long afternoon of apologizing to my mother and the Winters for the destruction of property, I am exhausted and ready for another drink and some sleep.

Just as I reach for the bottle I hid under the bed, my phone buzzes. Nobody texts me anymore, so I'm taken aback for a second at the sound. My supposed friends from college dropped me after the "accident". Apparently, being friends with the girl who is not allowed to party anymore is not very appealing.

I pull my phone out only to be more surprised than I already was. It's Dylan.

Hey Miranda, sorry to bug you but I'm outside under the pine. Got a sec?

He is outside? Now?! He is probably here to find out why I washed his girlfriend's tablet. I sprint out the front door with the speed of an Olympian.

The sun has already set and I find Dylan standing by the pine, arms folded, head tilted up gazing at the stars. While he admires their beauty, the starlight traces his face, admiring his.

"Uh, hey, Dylan. What's up?" I know I look crazy and it only takes a second for me to remember that I am not wearing a bra, so I cross my arms over my chest to shield myself.

"Hey. Sorry to bug you, you weren't asleep already, were you?"

"No, it's fine. Is this about the tablet?"

"What? Oh. That. No. Not really. I got a text from Diego asking me to check on you because you weren't responding to him anymore. I think he's worried . . . are you blowing him off or something?"

"Oh, uh, yeah. I guess I am. I haven't really felt like talking to anyone lately."

"Is everything okay?" Dylan sounds sincere and it kills me. He has to stop caring about me, otherwise getting over him will be impossible.

"Sure. Yeah, it's all good."

"Is this about tomorrow?" He *remembered?*

"No, not at all. You remember when my birthday is?"

"Of course, I remember. I spent every birthday with you for like eight years, how could I forget?"

I shrug, "Fair enough."

"Well, it'd be wrong not to celebrate with you being here and all. Why don't we have Diego and Jebb come up tomorrow and we can have a bonfire like we used to? It might be nice. We can make it more of a party if you want. I can ask them to bring some friends."

My brittle heart leaps inside my chest. Celebrate my birthday like we used to? My excitement is immediate and overwhelming, but I try to appear unaffected.

"Sure. That would be cool. I mean, it's no big deal."

"I don't know, birthdays are important. Come over tomorrow night and I'll take care of the rest."

"Okay, see you then."

"See you, May. Sorry, I meant Miranda. Old habits die hard." I smile because he does not realize how much I hate it when he calls me Miranda and for a split-second, I consider telling him to stop.

He turns and walks away with his hands in his pockets. I watch him for longer than I care to admit.

An unfamiliar sensation is filling the cracks in my heart. It takes a moment for me to recognize it as hope.

The next day is torture. I'm so excited to celebrate my birthday back on the ranch like I used to that I stare at the clock waiting for minutes to tick by. I promised myself when I got up this morning that I would stay sober until I got to the party, but by five o'clock, I'm so anxious that I have to have a couple glasses of wine just to calm my nerves.

The sun is almost set when I finally leave the house and make my way to the Ryder Ranch. It's a windless night which is perfect for a bonfire. As I round the road and the ranch comes into view, I can see a stream of smoke drifting into the darkening sky behind the Ryder's house. The peace that comes over me is unexpected.

I feel safe and for the first time in years, I feel like I'm finally *home*.

Chapter Twenty-Eight

Dylan

I really did not want to invite Diego to May's birthday but I cannot find any way around it. Candace is watching everything I do like a hawk and I know that she will read too much into it if I don't invite him.

Maybe she would be right to read into it. The idea of seeing them hang out or touch each other, on her birthday of all days, is unbearable but I have to get over it.

When Diego and Jebb arrive, they bring four of their friends with them. Two of them I know from around town, the other two are out-of-towners. It is a chill crowd, but I can tell they are the type that like to party. Part of me is glad, I want May to let loose and have a good time tonight, but another part of me is worried about her drinking. I will do my best to try to keep an eye on her tonight and get her home safely.

The crowd heads right inside to eat the dinner my mother has cooked when they get here. They are all extremely excited for my mother's legendary barbeque pulled pork sandwiches. I told her that I would take care of it. She is so tired of late that I did not want her to exhaust herself, but she insisted, saying she always cooked for May's birthday and wanted to again.

After I spoke with May by the creek, I tried to get up the courage to confront my mom about her health, but I backed out at the last moment. Really, I'm terrified of what she might say. I reason with myself that if it was serious, she would have told me by now, but I'm not sure that's true.

It is almost dark out and the bonfire is blazing so May should be here soon. I thought about getting her a gift, but I am pretty sure Candace would have my head on a chopping block, so I refrain.

I'm alone by the fire when I hear footsteps behind me. I turn my head and see May walking towards me and I'm taken aback.

She's *smiling*.

Not just any smile either, but a May smile, and it is just like the ones she had when we were kids. A moment of déjà vu hits me like a wave and a vision plays behind my eyes.

The dark of night is soft as the sun ducks behind the horizon. The stars have begun to twinkle but are still fuzzy to the naked eye. I wait patiently for May to arrive. We are going to set up a small campfire to make s'mores and play cards. I just got a new deck and am anxious to break them in. Plus, I love playing with May because she is just as competitive as I am.

I hear footsteps approaching so I turn my head and see her walking towards me; suddenly my heart stops and takes an agonizing amount of time before starting again. The smile that spreads across her face is so beautiful I have to remind myself to breathe.

Then it happens. The realization that I have always known but never fully understood.

I'm in love with this girl. I always knew I loved her, but the love I'm feeling right now is a much bigger love than I thought possible. I know in this moment that one day, years from now, she will be my wife. She will be my everything.

My fragile thirteen-year-old heart can barely handle the realization and I have to pump my hand to my chest to get it to start beating again before I die right here and now.

"Dylan?" May's voice startles me back from the

memory with a slap. "You okay? You have a weird look on your face."

"Uh, oh. Yeah, no, I'm good. Um, happy birthday." I try to smile at her but my face has started to hurt.

"Thanks. I love the fire, great job. It's even better than how I remember." As May goes on about how excited she is for this night, my head swarms with the gnawing awareness that I am still completely in love with the person standing in front of me.

That I never stopped.

I excuse myself abruptly. I have to get away before I fall apart completely.

I can't.

I just can't. She will hurt me again and this time, I'm not sure I'll ever recover when she does.

Chapter Twenty-Nine

Miranda

Dylan looks mortified when I approach him. My excitement fades immediately. *Should I not have come? Did he regret saying he would do this?* He almost looks sick as he scurries away, leaving me alone by the bonfire that is mocking me with its flames.

Broken pieces of hope crumble inside my now empty chest.

He will never forgive me. We will never be the same. We will never be close again. He does not even like to be around me anymore. I am invisible. I have no one. *I am nothing.*

With a renewed hate for myself and my life, I run inside to get the only thing that ever seems to make me feel better.

I don't know how long I have been here. Time has become hazy thanks to the four shots of vodka from Mrs. Ryder's liquor cabinet that I drink in secret and the entire bottle of wine that I chugged. Now, onto the second bottle, it will not be long; I should be completely numb and I cannot wait for it.

Candace has been glaring at me this entire time, her bleached hair making it look like she has a ring of fire around her stupid face. Diego has been at my side almost every second. He keeps touching me but I'm no longer capable of pretending to like it.

Mrs. Ryder went to bed a little while ago and trusts us to be safe down here. I love her but she can be so naïve.

I have made friends, though, with two of the people Diego and Jebb brought. They are from out of town and are visiting for the weekend. The one wearing flannel has a flask in his pocket, so I know I'm with the right kind of people. My college ways come back in full force and party girl Miranda is out to play.

Leaning against the countertop, I take a shot of whisky with my new friends. They erupt into cheers. I glance around and notice Dylan for the first time since he left me by the bonfire. He's sitting on a chair outside facing away from me.

I watch in slow motion as Candace makes her way over to him, running her hand through his hair as she sits down on his lap, his arms wrapping around her waist as she does.

The once empty chest of mine is no longer empty and begins to fill with liquor and something else—something sticky and bitter.

Time freezes all around me, silence fills my ears as I watch him tilt his head back while she leans forward. She plants her lips on his. A peck turns into an open-mouthed kiss and what is left of my world, collapses into ashes.

Before I can think, I do the unthinkable.

I smash my wine glass on to the floor.

Red liquid and fragments of glass shoot everywhere. Diego steps back quickly, cursing as he does. The noise from the collision of glass against hardwood ends the kiss I never wanted to see. Dylan and Candace jump up and run inside towards the source of the sound. Dylan is clearly worried as he searches everyone's faces for an explanation.

Slowly, the eyes in the room land on me.

My hands are gripped so tightly that the nails of my fingers are digging painfully into my palms.

"Are you okay, May? What's happened?" Dylan

approaches cautiously, as though I am a wild animal. At this moment, he is right.

"Did you tell your precious girlfriend about us?" Hate fills me to the top, overflowing onto the floor and spreading like a disease.

Dylan scrunches his face in confusion and recognition, "How much have you had to drink?"

"It doesn't matter. I want to know if you've told her about us."

"What are you talking about, Miranda?" Oh, so we are back to Miranda now. I see he is starting to get angry. *Good.*

"That we kissed before she got here? That you're obsessed with me." An audible gasp comes from everyone in the room.

Dylan shoves his hands in his front pockets and urges Candace not to say anything. I can't hear everything he says to her because my head is so cloudy, but I think he mentions to her he will explain later.

"Miranda, you're wasted. You need to go home. Let Diego walk you." This only makes me hate him more.

"Come on, Miranda, I'll take you home." Diego reaches for me and I push him away.

"Stay away from me. I don't even like you!" I scream this at Diego, going for the most damage. The hurt in Diego's face is unmistakable but, in this moment, I don't care. I barely notice that he grabs his keys and leaves out the front door.

"You know, Dylan, I never really liked you. I thought you were so pathetic. All those letters you wrote me. I told you I didn't read them, but I did. You are such a whiny baby. I took them to school and showed them to everyone. We laughed about it all the time. You were so weird and annoying. I can't believe I ever tried to be friends with you again." No longer able to control the octave of my voice, I go from yelling to talking back to yelling before I can finish spewing all of my hatred towards him.

I thought I would feel relieved to have hurt him, but the jolt of grief that strikes his face is not relieving at all, instead, it is an awakening.

Oh, no. What have I done?

Panicked, I turn and flee out the front door, leaving everything behind. I don't even grab my phone.

As soon as I reach my house, tears are streaming down my face. An overwhelming sensation of breathlessness takes over. I clutch my chest and bolt directly for the wine cellar.

It is here in this quiet place on top of a mountain that my world goes dark.

Chapter Thirty

Dylan

My knuckles are white from gripping the sides of the bathroom vanity while cool water drips off my face.

After leaving May at the bonfire, I came into this bathroom to splash water on my face hoping it would rinse away the throbbing in my head. My hands are trembling while I rub a towel over myself.

I do not want to feel this way. *I can't.* I do not want to be in love with May. She has devasted me so profoundly in the past that the idea of going through that causes tremors to skate up my back into the base of my neck.

What am I going to do?

Nobody can see me.

Standing outside by the window on the front porch, I can see them, but they don't see me. I watch quietly as May sneaks vodka out of my mom's liquor cabinet and takes multiple shots. She then slurps down so much wine I'm surprised she is still standing. Candace is pouting with her arms crossed in the corner while everyone else remains oblivious to anything that is going on. Diego lurks like a creep.

I have no idea how to handle this situation.

If I try to get May to go home, Candace will be all over me, and in reality, May is not mine. If she wants to get drunk like this, she can.

Candace is blowing up my phone wanting to know where I am, so I leave my hiding spot to sit by the bonfire. I do not really want to watch as May gets drunk, anyway.

"Hey, there you are."

"Hey."

"What've you been doing?" Candace says this in a whiny voice, and I notice for the first time just how annoying it is.

"Sorry, I had to take care of some stuff with the animals. You having fun?"

"Not at all." Candace closes in and sits on my lap. I would rather she didn't, but I don't have any real reason to push her away. I just hope May does not see.

"Come here," she purrs so I tilt my head up and she comes in for a kiss before I can think twice. I should not feel guilty about kissing my own girlfriend, but for some cruel reason—I do.

Crash.

The sound causes us both to bolt out of the chair and run into the house.

It's eerie. No one is moving and May is standing over broken glass and wine. I would have thought it was just a mistake but by the hateful look on her face, I can tell it was on purpose. She is so angry her face has turned bright red and her fists are clenched.

As I approach, knowing this is not going to be good, it occurs to me that she could see Candace and I perfectly from where she is standing. Is that why she did this? Because we were kissing?

I try to tell her calmly that she needs to go home and when Diego steps in to take her home, she shoves him back. He is not hurt, but his ego is, and he bolts out of the house.

Next, she turns her attack on me. She tries to throw me under the bus for the kiss in the tent, then proceeds to tear me apart. She says she read my letters, calls me pathetic, and my heart fills with embarrassment and contempt, but before I can respond, she's gone.

I let her leave.

We all do.

Jebb and the rest of the others leave without a word, other than a "Whoa, that was awkward."

Candace is furious and stomps away upstairs toward the bedroom. I should run after her but I have to clean up this mess first.

"Dylan? What happened? I heard yelling." My mom is up, standing in the kitchen in her long sweatpants and t-shirt. She looks frail but I brush it aside, not wanting to dwell on it.

"Sorry, Mom. I don't know what happened really. May got mad and broke a wine glass. I think she was just really drunk. I'll clean it up."

"Is it true you two kissed?"

I sigh, "I was hoping you didn't hear any of that."

"What's going on, Dylan?"

I look up the stairs to make sure Candace has not come back down before telling my mother the truth, "We did kiss. The night we had to stay on the mountain when we were looking for Sally. It was just a one-time thing."

"Mmm." Mom says this while handing me the broom and paper towels. "Sounds kind of complicated, Dylan. Who initiated it?"

"She did."

"Who stopped it?"

"I did."

"Why?"

"Mom, Candace is right upstairs. I can't really talk about this."

"Dylan, forget Candace for a moment and try to be honest with me, with yourself."

"I stopped it because of Candace, of course."

"Is that really why?" I really wish my mother was not

so perceptive.

I take a deep breath, then try again, "No, not really. The truth is that I wanted to kiss her, too, but I can't. She broke my heart, Mom. I can't go down the May path again. It just leads to pain."

"You are only hurting yourself and your potential happiness by not forgiving her, Dylan. She was a young girl who was hurt by what was happening with her parents. I'm not saying it wasn't a crappy thing for her to do, but is there really no way you can forgive her? We're not all perfect people, Dylan. We all make mistakes. Don't you think that she deserves a second chance?"

"Why do you care so much if I forgive her or not, Mom?"

She leans against the counter, watching me wipe up the spilled wine, "I just know how much she means to you, Dylan. You've loved that girl since you were six years old. It seems a waste to throw it all away."

"I didn't throw it away, she did."

"Yes, but she's here now trying to make amends and you're the one throwing her away. How's what you're doin' any better than what she did to you?"

I sit on the wooden floor, resting my elbows on my knees. I do not know what to say to my mom. Maybe she's right. At this moment, I just don't know. She turns and heads back to her bedroom, leaving me alone in this kitchen with a broken glass and a broken heart.

Chapter Thirty-One

Dylan

I will not go check on her.
I will not go check on her.
It would be crazy to go check on her.

I repeat this manta as Candace snores lightly beside me. She did not want to go back to May's after the debacle, which is understandable. After a very long discussion about the kiss in the tent, she finally settled down, but when she tried to have make-up sex with me, I just couldn't do it. I blamed a headache but—really—I'm just too worried about May to think about anything else right now.

Even after she spewed all her hate at me, I'm still worried about her. She's right—I am pathetic. I cannot stop thinking about how much she has been drinking and start to worry that she might have alcohol poisoning and has passed out in her own vomit.

I keep thinking about what my mom said to me, too. Is she right? Am I doing to May what she did to me all those years ago? Is it worth it? Should I forgive her? Should I risk my heart again?

Forcing my eyelids to close and with the help of counting sheep, I finally manage to drift to sleep, but when the vision of May walking towards me with that smile of hers enters my dreams, I wake up in a cold sweat.

I peel the comforter off my now wet skin and crawl out of the bed at a methodically slow pace, so I don't disturb Candace. My feet have shoes on them and are out the front door headed in the direction of May before I can stop them. My head keeps trying to get them to turn back around and go back to bed, but gives up the struggle after a few steps into the cool mountain air.

The stillness of the night ushers a calm wave over me.

At least I will be able to sleep once I know she's okay.

The house is dark and the driveway is empty except for May's Subaru, but this is not a surprise. Candace's parents got tired of the quiet life of the mountains after a couple of weeks and have been spending their nights in town enjoying the local poker games and dive bars. Candace says they are out all night most of the time now.

I step up onto the front porch, desperately trying to come up with a plan on what I am going to say if May is awake, but these thoughts fall away when I notice the front door is open.

Odd.

I pull open the screen and walk inside. It becomes apparent that the front door is not the only thing that is out of place.

I can hear a faint wheezing-like sound.

What is that?

I turn on the living room light and glance around. I don't see May anywhere. I make my way towards her bedroom door down the hall when I hear the sound again. Turning toward where the sound is coming from—my heart short circuits.

A soft light is trinkling through a sliver of open door to the wine cellar.

Oh no.

She should not be down there.

Something's not right.

My feet move so fast—I'm practically flying as I push the door wide open—the sound of it hitting the stone cellar wall is loud, but I barely notice it as I pound down the stairs.

I see her instantly.

Curled in the fetal position on the floor, there are

bottles of wine laying haphazardly around her small form, along with some shards of glass, and she is completely motionless. The soft wheezing coming from her tells me that she is still alive.

I'm on my knees beside her, reaching for her when I see it.

I assume it's wine.

Red wine—to be exact—as it flows onto my hand while I cradle her body and call out her name.

But it's not.

It's not wine.

Chapter Thirty-Two

Miranda

You know those moments in your life where you knew nothing would ever be the same after?

Those moments that end up being critical junctures in the timeline of your life—altering your path indefinitely for better or for worse?

We have all had those moments, some are just bigger than others. The small ones are less obvious—like spending summers running through a field of sunflowers—but no less impactful. For instance, the love that I developed for the landscape of my home in the Colorado Rockies has defined a large part of who I am, and in ways that I may never fully understand.

The big ones, though, those are different. Those are the ones you remember. Those are the ones you tell your therapist about. They can be good and bad, like your wedding day or the birth of a child or when you lose a loved one.

For me, the big ones have not only altered the course of my life, but fractured it.

One of them is obvious: my parents' divorce.

I have others, though. Other moments that are worse. Some so painful I have tried to bury them as though they never happened.

The night of my twenty-first birthday is one of these moments.

One of the big ones.

Maybe even the biggest one of them all.

I do not remember much.

When I wake up in a hospital bed some indiscernible amount of time later, my parents are there and they both have this unusual look streaked across their faces. A look I have never seen on either of them before. It is hard to describe, but I assume that it is the type of look that only occurs when you mix shock and sorrow.

My mother's eyes are rimmed with a faint red color and puffy from obvious crying. My father—well, he just looks like has not slept in days.

"Miranda? Dear? Can you hear us?"

"Where am I?" I ask groggily. The weight of my body making it hard to talk.

"You're in the hospital. Do you remember what happened?"

"No, was I in an accident?" My father glances quickly to my mother and I know then that I'm not going to like what they say.

"No, Miranda," his voice is deep and firm, "you were not in an accident. You got really drunk and apparently took a piece of broken glass and tried to slit your wrists in our wine cellar."

"What?!"

Then it all floods back, or at least parts of it.

I remember the pain in my chest. I remember the overwhelming despair. I remember the wine cellar. I think I may have dropped one of the bottles by accident but when I picked up a broken shard, I took it as a sign, an opportunity to end it all—the suffering.

"You're lucky Dylan found you when he did. The doctor said that if you had lost any more blood, you would have—" My father's voice cracks as he chokes on his words. His eyes swell with tears while mine fill with guilt. I have never seen my father cry and I certainly do not want to be the cause of it.

"Dylan? Dylan found me? How?"

"He said you caused a scene at your birthday party and so he knew you had drank a lot. He was worried about you so he went over to check on you. He said he found you on the floor of the wine cellar. It was a couple of hours after you had left . . . He's called your mother at least fifty times since you got here yesterday. He's very concerned. You know, you have a lot of people who love and care for you . . . what's going on, Miranda? How could you do something like this?"

As my grief-stricken parents' stare at me with more intensity than they ever have before, I know that I'm in for a long and difficult journey ahead.

Chapter Thirty-Three

Dylan

Exhaustion rakes over my body with its long and heavy fingers.

The lack of sleep from worrying about May is taking its toll. I have probably aged ten years in two days.

I call Lynn more times than I can count desperate for updates. I kept thinking *what if? What if this is it? What if she doesn't come back from this? What if I never get to speak to her again? What if she's gone?* When May finally regained consciousness yesterday, I started to feel like I could breathe again—but just barely.

When I found her in the wine cellar, it took me a moment to understand what I was seeing. The red liquid all over the ground around her was a mix of red wine and blood. It was only when I picked up her hand and saw the blood seeping from a jagged cut in her skin, that I fully understood what was going on.

Shock is a strange thing.

My body went into emergency mode and my brain went blank. I remember picking up her small body and carrying her out to the Subaru. I vaguely remember thinking that I was glad the keys to the car were stored in the center console, in the same place that May's parents used to leave them when we were kids. I remember fastening May's seatbelt as her body slumped forward in the passenger seat. At some point, apparently, I tore the t-shirt off that I was wearing under my hoodie and wrapped it around both of her wrists to try to stop the bleeding, but I don't actually remember doing all of that. My mind became a foggy state of confusion and focus. Focused on getting her to the hospital, but not fully aware of anything else. My mother says I called her from the car. She says I sounded lost and just kept saying "she's going to die" and "how could this happen?"

I do remember driving fast. So fast that I was grateful nobody else was on that mountain road because I might not have been able to slow down. I didn't have a choice. It can take an ambulance a long time to get up this far and she had already lost so much blood.

I only took my eyes off the road once—this I will never forget—and it was to look over to the passenger seat. There she was, slumped forward, blood was gushing from wrists, soaking through the shirt haphazardly wrapped around her arms. Her face was gray and her hair was stuck to her face. Her skin was clammy and wet, causing a sheen all over her exposed skin. Her mouth was slightly ajar, and her eyes were shut. It was too loud in the car to hear her breathing. I would have thought she was dead, but since she was still bleeding, I had hope.

The image of her dying body will forever be imprinted on my brain. I will see it for the rest of my life. After I looked once, I didn't make that mistake again and focused on the road.

When I flew into the small hospital parking lot on the edge of town, I was greeted by surprised hospital staff. Not a lot of emergencies happen in a place like this and we were the only people in the emergency department that night.

My mother called Lynn who called May's dad who both got on a plane and arrived early the following morning, while my mom and I sat in the waiting room all night, not wanting to leave until they got there.

I do not cry a lot. I never have. I can count on one hand how many times I have cried in the last ten years and I did not cry that night in the hospital, either.

I *sobbed*.

My head swarmed with painful questions. *Did I do*

this? Was this my fault? What could I have done to prevent this? Why would she do this? How did I not see this coming?

The guilt is nauseating—not allowing me to sleep or eat.

My mother has been hovering ever since we got home from the hospital, not wanting to leave my side. I can hear her climbing the stairs now headed towards my room so she can check on me yet again.

"Dyl? Sweetie? Are you asleep?"

I groan. "No, I'll probably never sleep again."

"Get up, dear. It's almost noon and I need you to tend to the horses."

"I can't, Mom."

"Please, son. It'll be good for you. You can't just lay around this room wallowing in misery. May is okay. She's going to be okay. She's alive and that's all that matters. I just spoke to Lynn this morning and she said that they have entered her into a treatment facility for addiction and mental health issues. They will help her. There's nothing more you can do, Dylan."

I sit on the edge of my bed with my head in my hands. "I know, but I just feel so guilty, Mom." I barely recognize my own voice.

"You have no reason to feel guilty. You didn't cause this, in fact, you saved her life, Dylan. Without you, we would've lost her."

"I've been so mad at her. I should've been nicer to her. I should've insisted she tell me what was wrong when I caught her drinking that first time. But I didn't. I was too concerned about myself and how she hurt me years ago. It all seems so stupid now."

"I know, son. But now you have another chance. Make it up to her. Tell her you forgive her for what happened when you were kids and be her friend. She needs your friendship now more than ever." Her hand rubs my back in slow circles, comforting me as she always has.

I exhale a long breath, "Okay Mom. I will."

Candace and I never technically break up.

The Winters went home the next day after what happened with May. Candace has not spoken to me since. She realized it was over when she found out that I slipped out of the house that night without telling her to go check on May.

I know I should call her and explain, and apologize. To be honest, I'm nervous to. How do I explain? How can I explain to her that I've been in love with May for my entire life and that I'm sorry that I lied to her about it—lied to myself?

Candace beats me to it and surprises me with a text.

I put down the brush that I was using to comb out Sally's coat to read the message.

Hey, I just wanted to let you know before you hear it from someone else that I have starting dating someone. Sorry. Hope you can recover. I don't mean to hurt you.

I pick up my phone and text back. Giving her the apology that she deserves.

Hey, I'm glad you're dating someone new. I want you to be happy. I know I was not a good boyfriend to you and I'm sorry. You deserve better than how I treated you.

She never responds. I pick the brush back up and all my thoughts drift back to May.

Chapter Thirty-Four

Miranda

Treatment is brutal.

My days consist of individual therapy, group therapy, withdrawal management, and nothing else. No television, no phone, no nothing. To make matters worse, I have to share my room with Lizzy, a meth addict who only has three teeth and looks about twenty years older than twenty-five like she claims to be. She snores so loud that it sounds like sirens are in our room.

My parents found me a treatment facility back in Vermont so that they could be close by and available to come for family therapy sessions.

The only real upside is that it is peaceful here. The facility is a large brick building tucked away on forty acres of wooded land. The sycamore trees that dot the landscape outside my window are undoubtably beautiful, however, nothing compares to the mountains, the pine, and aspen trees, and—of course—the sunflowers.

It has been one week into my six weeks stay and right now I'm at my worst. No longer able to use alcohol to numb my brain and keep painful thoughts at bay, the intrusive memories are pushing their way to the surface unobstructed.

I know what's coming. I have always known. There was going to come a point when I was going to have to talk about what happened; talk about one of the moments—one of the big ones.

In therapy, I start with getting kicked out of college and the night I drove my car into the tree, but my therapist, Dr. Wright, is smarter than that and keeps pushing me to dig deeper. She wants me to really understand what the trauma is that I'm hiding from. What is it that is making living so hard?

I know what she wants to know. I know, but I'm afraid to tell her. If I talk about it out loud, then it becomes real and that's why I have never told a single person.

After it happened, my brain tried to erase it completely. No matter what I do, though, it is still there—festering inside me.

Dr. Wright refuses to let me ignore it. I guess this is what makes her a good therapist.

"Miranda, from your own admission, you have attempted suicide on two separate occasions. I suspect that something is going on that you have never dealt with. A trauma you are trying to avoid. In order to heal, really heal and move forward with your life, you have to work through that trauma. Please talk to me. Tell me what happened. Can we start there?"

It surprises me how much I like Dr. Wright. She has a face full of soft features and big chestnut eyes that remind me of Dylan. With her short stature and oversized jewelry, she is almost comical. It is her smile that I like the most. It's genuine and causes her eyes to crinkle at the sides. With this bit of encouragement, and the crushing desire to get my life back on track, I decide to trust her and share my story.

So, I start at the beginning.

I tell her all about Dylan, the kiss on the boulder as kids, the divorce, and how I cut him out of my life for many years.

She is intuitive, she digs further, "What kinds of things did you do during your teen years, Miranda? After the divorce? After Dylan? Did you have friends? When did the drinking start?"

"I started drinking when I was fifteen at my birthday party. It was the first birthday party I didn't spend on the mountain since I was six years old. I think I was missing it and wanted to forget. My friend Sam snuck a bottle of tequila into my mom's house and after she went to sleep, we drank it. All of it. And I liked it. I liked how it made me feel. I guess that was the beginning, the rest of my sophomore and junior year, I was partying. I was partying all the time. By the age of seventeen, I was Stanford High's most notorious party girl."

Dr. Wright lifts her left eyebrow at this. She encourages me to keep talking by remaining silent. It's a good technique.

"My first real boyfriend was Peter. I liked him because he didn't judge me when I partied, he encouraged it. He was a year older than me and I guess I trusted him to keep me safe, but in retrospect, I should've known better."

"Tell me more about what happened with Peter. You said you trusted him to keep you safe, what happened that made you feel unsafe?"

This is the hard part. The truth. Dr. Wright hands me a tissue. Without noticing, I had started to cry. A silent cry. What is left of my fractured heart is lodged against my ribs, threatening to break through my chest.

"Take a minute before telling me. Breathe deep and let it out, Miranda. I promise you, once you unload what you're carrying around, you'll begin to feel better."

She is right, I can feel it. So, I unload the whole awful truth.

I explain how Peter was becoming increasingly frustrated with me because I kept refusing his sexual advances. I kept saying I was not ready, but he could not understand that. What he didn't know was that I did not want to give myself to anyone—not completely. After the divorce, I knew that I was destined for heartbreak unless I kept my guard up and kept myself from falling in love, and it was easy with Peter because I didn't love him. I liked to party with him, but that was it. So, I assumed I was safe from any real pain.

I was wrong.

In movies and books, losing your virginity is often glamourized as something special. Some sacred moment that you will hold on to for the rest of your life. Something that is memorable, sweet, gentle, and with someone who really cares about you. In reality, that is not always the case and it certainly wasn't for me.

I was not even awake during my first time. I was passed out in Peter's bed after a drinking bender.

It was my seventeenth birthday and we had been in a fight early in the night. He wanted to have sex to celebrate and I had told him no again. I remember him saying that we were done and that he didn't want to be with me anymore. I remember him being angry about it. He had thrown a party at his place and bought me all the booze I wanted and I owed him. He had made sure his parents were going to be out of town for the weekend and even arranged for his twenty-two-year-old brother who was back from college to supply the party with the liquor. He had spent a lot of money on the alcohol and I needed to make it up to him. I remember refusing and grabbing some more drinks and partying well into the night.

The next thing I remember, I was waking up.

It is with Dr. Wright's kind eyes on mine, that I take a shaky breath and allow the memory to flood to the surface, washing over me completely.

My eyes crack open slowly—it hurts to blink, so I try to ease myself into sitting up and look around. I spend a moment trying to remember where I am. I recognize it as Peter's room. I glide my hand down my chest and realize that I'm naked. Completely and totally naked. I glance around to see if I am alone and I am. I have no idea what happened last night but an unfamiliar soreness is sitting between my legs. I pull the sheet back and see dark staining—blood, I think. That is when I see the crumped and used condom lying next to me.

I grab my t-shirt and shorts, dressing frantically.

I look everywhere, the kitchen, bathroom, bedrooms, but can't find Peter anywhere inside of the house. I run outside, out the back sliding doors, to see if he is sleeping in a lounge chair by the pool. That is where the majority of the party took place so I think I might find him there.

And I do. I find him.

He is sound asleep with a women wrapped around him. It's Sam. They look like they might be naked underneath a pool towel with sharks printed on it draped over them haphazardly. For a second, I am pissed at her. I thought she was one of my best friends, but that thought leaves quickly as full-blown fear takes its place, causing my heart to pound heavily in my chest, slamming violently against my ribcage as the blood in my body heats to an unhealthy degree.

If he is out here with her, then who spent the night with me? Who did I have sex with?

I need to get out of here. NOW.

I turn around and race back into the house. I find my phone and call for a ride. As I turn the corner of the banister at the top of the staircase, an arm wraps around my waist.

It is him. The older brother.

I can't even think of his name right now, but he is grinning wide at me like we are well acquainted.

"Where you going, birthday girl?"

"Home." Please let me go, I plead internally.

"Cool. Last night was a blast, I hope you enjoyed your birthday present."

The man in front of me, slightly pudgy with ruffled

blond hair and crooked teeth, licks his lips and squeezes my waist with an unwelcome arm. His hands are clammy and cold against my skin.

Dread hits me and sinks to the soles of my feet.

"What present?" But I already know. I already know what I don't want to know.

"The gift of taking your virginity, of course. Don't worry, girlie, Peter told me he didn't want you anymore, so I was free to have ya'. And have ya' I did." He is laughing now. He finds something funny about this situation but I have no idea what.

"I don't remember that." My voice cracks with these words.

"Well, you weren't fully awake the entire time, but the moments you were you seemed to be enjoying it." His crooked grin is proud, like he is saying something to be proud of.

"You can't do that. You can't have sex with someone who isn't awake. That's illegal." I was shaking my head like I can't quite accept what was going on.

For the first time, he frowns. "It's your word against mine, girlie, and Peter's got my back. So, who's going to believe you—the party girl? If you know what's good for you, you'll say you liked it and move on."

Was he right? If both he and Peter said it was consensual will anyone believe me? Everyone loved Peter, he was the fun one. The popular one. Who was I? Just the girl who got too drunk at her birthday party?

I glance back up from the now crumbled tissue squeezed between my fingers and find the warm and sympathetic face of Dr. Wright. When I start to cry harder and blame myself for what happened, she reaches for my hand and squeezes gently.

"No, Miranda. This is not your fault. You were taken

advantage of. You were sexually assaulted. You had sex without being able to give consent. Only one person is responsible for his actions that night, and it is the person who assaulted you. Period. I will help you work through this; you will get through this but I need you to be willing to put in the work."

Over the next five weeks, that's exactly what I do.

Trauma can control you and change how you view the world. It can define you and every choice you make for the rest of your life.

I have many epiphanies while in rehab, none of which are easy. Recognizing that I use alcohol to cope with my trauma is just the surface. Accepting that I'm a selfish person who puts her own needs first while lying to every person in her life is one of the hardest things that I have realized about myself. Learning how to become a better person is not a simple process, complicated by my understanding of my own trauma and addiction.

On what seemed like a normal Tuesday in individual therapy with Dr. Wright, something happens. I experience an epiphany that would change me, putting me on a new path. This moment seemed small at first, but I later learned was one of the big ones.

"Miranda—"

"Doc, please call me May. It's the name I used to go by and I would like to go by it again."

"Okay, May—I'm going to tell you something that I think you need to hear, to really hear. Listen to my words carefully. The trauma you have experienced does not have to define who you are. Did you hear me? Let me repeat that, the trauma you have experienced does not have to define who you are. These moments, from your parents' divorce to the sexual assault, impacted you, yes. They changed the direction of your life, yes. However, you have come to let them define who you are and they don't have to. You get to define who you are. Do you understand what I mean by that?"

I think for a moment on what she says. I'm not sure I understand, "What do you mean? How could they not define who I am. I'm a child of divorce, a victim of sexual assault."

"Yes, May. These things happened *to* you, but they are not who you are. You are May, daughter, friend, and lover of the Colorado Rockies. You are May, witty and smart with a sensitive heart. You are not just May, victim. Think about my words, May. Leave therapy today and think about it all night, about what I've said. When we talk again tomorrow, I want to hear what you think I mean by that."

Lying in bed hours later with Lizzy's raucous snoring filling this small room, I analyze Dr. Wright's words over and over and try to understand them. Then a memory comes into my mind and like a guiding light, it leads me to where I need to be.

It's Tuesday night and I'm at Dylan's. I'm waiting until Mrs. Ryder falls asleep so that I can sneak into Dylan's room. It's always the same thing. I wait and listen for Mrs. Ryder, while Dylan waits and listens for me. Tonight, though, I'm impatient. I want to talk to Dylan about our next adventure because I'm really excited about it. We have been discussing our plan to sneak out at night and carve our names into our boulder, but we are still sorting through the details of our plan. Sometimes planning our adventures is just as fun as the adventure themselves.

I crawl out of bed and slowly turn the knob to the door. I know Mrs. Ryder is not asleep yet because I do not hear her snoring, but I think I can slip past the door to her bedroom and into Dylan's without her noticing. I'm really good at sneaking around.

I do not make a sound as I inch my way down the hallway and into Dylan's room. Luckily, I am paying attention and do not just bust into Dylan's room the second I get to the door, because the door is open slightly and I can hear talking. I flatten myself to the wall and wait and listen. I want to know who is talking and what about. It only takes half of a second to recognize Mrs. Ryder's voice.

"It's okay, Dyl. Everything's okay. No need to cry. You should be happy, it's May's night to stay here and I know you love it when she stays." Crying? Dylan never cries. Suddenly my chest hurts with worry.

Sniff, "I know. Don't tell May I cried, Mom. I don't want her to think I'm a pansy."

Mrs. Ryder laughs quietly before responding, "No problem, dear. I won't tell her."

"I just can't help it, Mom. I thought about dad today and it made me so sad."

"What made you think of him, Dyl?"

"I was brushing Sally and she rested her head on my shoulder when I did. You told me once that Sally loved Dad, is that true? Did she ever rest her head on his shoulder like she did today on mine?"

A pause, "Yes, as a matter of fact, she did. She used to do that all of the time. I think she loves you just as much as she loved your dad. She was the first horse we ever got when we bought this place, you know."

"What was he like, Mom? I can't remember him. What was he like?"

"He was hilarious. You remind me so much of him.

Plus, you have his dimple. You and him are so much alike."

"I hate it. I hate that he's not here with us. I hate not having a dad. Will it ever get better? Will it ever stop hurting so much?"

"Yes, Dyl. Losing your dad hurt and it will always be with you, but that does not mean that you can't be happy, that you can't be okay. It's important that you understand that. You need to mourn him when it feels right to, like today, but don't hold on to it. He would not want your life to be all about losing him. Your life is bigger than that."

It dawns on me what Dr. Wright wants me to understand. I am more than what has happened to me, we are all more than the individual moments of our lives. We are so much more and we get to decide who we are and who we want to be.

I, May, do not want to be an alcoholic, or a selfish girl who hurts those that she loves. I, May, do not want to be consumed by pain caused by predators. I, May, do not want to allow the hurt that happened from my parents' divorce to stop me from believing in love. I, May, am a woman who loves the mountains, sunflowers, believes in magic, and who loves a boy, the same boy she has loved all her life. She is kind and loving and smart. She is a good person.

A smile tugs at my mouth for the first time since my twenty-first birthday party and I let it take hold, allowing happiness and pride to overcome the bitter pain that I have allowed to sit in my chest for so long.

It's time. Time for me to be happy.

Chapter Thirty-Five

May

Out of everything that happens in treatment, family therapy is the most emotionally draining. I know it is necessary but it is so hard to see the pain on my parents faces as they try to understand what has been going on with me.

Each week, both of my parents show up to meet with me and Dr. Wright. It is gut-wrenching to hear them cry about how worried they are for me and how shocking the suicide attempts are for them.

It is here, with the help of Dr. Wright, that they learn about the assault when I was seventeen. I did not want to tell them about this but because I was underage at the time, and because my parents are still so involved in my recovery, Dr. Wright encouraged me to do so.

Honestly, unloading the burden and sharing this truth with my parents immediately makes me feel lighter—the guilt of keeping this secret for so long has been weighing me down more than I ever knew. In an unexpected way, sharing this with people who love me, sets me free. My parents handle it as one would expect, with a flood of emotions. Anger becomes the most dominant, taking them over in a way I have never seen before. After a lot of conversation, many tears, and pleading from my parents, I agree to consider filing charges. There is no statute of limitation for sex crimes in the state of Vermont, so even though it has been four years since the incident, I still have the ability to take some legal action. With the assault happening when I was still a minor, my dad volunteers to take the lead on speaking to a lawyer as soon as therapy is over today. I am nervous for what kind of stress filing charges might bring up, but Dr. Wright explains that it can be an important part of the healing process.

Today is important for healing and revelations but also happens to be my final family therapy session, and my final week of the in-patient treatment part of my recovery. In just a couple of days, I will be released to start an outpatient program which will consist of continued therapy and living with my mother.

When we finish the session—my parents thank Dr. Wright for all of her help, and my father heads outside to wait in the car because my mother asked for a moment alone with me. I love that they have been driving up here together for these meetings. It warms my heart that they are getting along so well.

Mom and I are walking back to my room—taking our time as we do. We are not talking and I'm patiently waiting for her to reveal whatever it is she needs to tell me.

"I brought you something, Ma—Miranda."

"It's okay, Mom, you can call me May. I want you to."

"Really?" Mom wraps her arm around my shoulder squeezing tight. "You just made my day."

I roll my eyes, but we are both smiling, "What did you bring me?"

"A gift—of sorts." I watch as she pulls out a bundle from her purse. When she hands it to me, I know instantly what it is, "You know I could never let you throw them away." With one more hug, she is gone, leaving me standing in the hallway with a handful of old letters.

Chapter Thirty-Six

Dylan

In the weeks that May is in rehab, things have gone from bad to worse at the ranch.

My mother's secret illness is now at the point where it can no longer be ignored. She is barely able to stay awake longer than a couple of hours at a time and only has an appetite for three granola bars a day. My anxiety around her health is made worse by the fact that she never talks about it. A part of me wants to continue in the weird state of not knowing and hoping that it isn't as bad as I suspect it is. I guess the saying *'ignorance is bliss'* has a ring of truth to it.

It's a hot Thursday afternoon when my bubble of ignorance is popped, and leaving my already broken heart, obliterated.

I'm coming inside the house from feeding the horses and cleaning the stables, but the second my foot crosses the threshold of the front door, I hear mom call for me.

"Dyl? Can you come here for a sec?" The tone of her voice is unusual, I can only recall hearing it once or twice before in my life. My throat constricts and my stomach bottoms out.

With a nervous pause, I answer. "Sure, Mom."

I walk slowly into the kitchen where I see Mom on her elbows bent over the granite countertop of the island. The windows are open in an attempt to cool down the house, but it has only seemed to make it warmer in here. A thundercloud is rolling in from the west and it's causing some shadows to skip across the floor by my feet.

Her long hair is falling over her shoulders, framing her now rail-thin face. I suck in a shaky breath and hold it as though it is the only thing keeping me together right now.

"Dyl. . . I know you know that I'm sick. I mean, it's obvious. I didn't want to tell you about it because I thought it'd be better for you to not have to worry about me. The time has come, though, where we can no longer ignore it."

"How bad is it?"

"Terminal. Cancer." The words that come out of her mouth are barely a whisper but they are the loudest words I have ever heard.

My jaw falls open with a million things to say, but nothing comes out.

"I'm so sorry, Dylan. I'm not ready to leave you yet. I wanted to be here for you for years to come, but the universe has other plans for me. Can you forgive me for not telling you?"

I can hear everything she is saying. I can see the pain etched in her face, but an unexpected emotion rips through me. *Rage.*

How *dare* she do this to me? How dare she leave me?

But then, that rage is quickly overtaken by something else, something worse. *Pain.*

My mom has tried to talk to me over the last couple of days, but I avoid her completely and I hate myself for it. I can't help it. I never knew it was possible to hurt like this. For pain to crawl over my skin and leave me weighted down with its misery.

After mom told me she was dying, I walked out of the house and went back to working on the ranch. My mind went blank. My thoughts about May, my mom, all of it, seeped out onto the dirt underneath my feet. In its place was just a sense of nothingness.

It has been two days and I am still completely lost and heartbroken. I'm sitting on the front porch now, watching the sun rise after another sleepless night, when the beauty of the world washes over me. A startling realization suddenly floods my consciousness: *My mom is almost out of sunrises.*

Overcome with panic, I race inside the house and up the stairs, throwing her bedroom door open. The door slams against the wall—jolting her awake.

"Dyl? What's wrong, dear?"

Tears flow freely now, soaking my face in a heaving cry.

"No, don't, Dylan. It's okay. It'll be okay, please come here."

I fall to my knees in front of her bed, my head in my hands. I can feel her wrap her tiny body around me as my shoulders shake in misery.

Chapter Thirty-Seven

May

The first letter I open from Dylan is the oldest one.

It's the one at the bottom of the stack. I'm amazed—and delighted—to have these in my possession. I never knew my mom kept these, but I should not be surprised. She has always been rooting for us.

With three more days left in rehab and six weeks almost behind me, I'm ready for what is next in my life, but I do have this nagging urge to go ahead and deal with the remaining components of my past that I have not dealt with yet: Dylan.

When my mother left yesterday and handed me this emotional bomb, I sat in my room and just stared at those letters before I got the nerve to read them—twelve hours later.

I wait for my strange roommate to leave the room—I need to be alone when I read these.

Memories of getting these letters flash into my mind. Once every couple of months, Mom would bring me a letter as they arrived in the mail, and I would respond each time she did with a "I don't want that. Throw it out."

My mother never took me seriously, though, because she always brought them to me anyway. Almost a year to the day after I left the ranch, she tried to hand me one last letter. I rejected it, again, and the letters stopped. A dark, deep place in my heart was irrationally hurt that he stopped writing, while on the surface, I acted like I didn't care.

The letters are all unopened. Relief swarms my limbs as I take note of this. The idea that anybody but me would see the words Dylan wrote me is gut wrenching. I have the overwhelming desire to keep him—and his words—safe and protected.

I am laying on my side with my head propped up on this very uncomfortable and flat pillow. My finger is tracing the edges of the old envelope, running over the handwritten address and my name.

At this point, I have even memorized the stamp—a columbine flower placed just askew on the right-hand corner.

I hesitate. Do I really want to read these? I know this is going to hurt. The dominant part of me knows that I *have* to read them, that it's a necessary part of my recovery. I just fear for my newly repaired heart.

It's as though there is a layer of emotional tape holding the pieces of me together, and reading these letters may cause that layer to disintegrate, but I do have hope. Hope that in its destruction, new, stronger pieces will take hold. This is just one of the lessons I will carry with me from this place, that by facing the pain head on, I can become stronger.

Delicately, I slowly glide my finger underneath the sealed edge and with the largest breath I have ever taken, I unfold the letter and allow the words to take over.

May- what happened? My mom said you had to leave because your parents are getting divorced but why didn't you tell me? Why didn't you say goodbye? I called your house a bunch but you won't call me back. I know you must be hurting, so maybe you just need space? I thought if I could write you like we normally do during the school year, that maybe you would write me back when you are ready? Or call me?

After you left, I went to your house the next day looking for you. I saw that your cars were gone and the house was locked up. I hope you're okay, May. I hope you know that I'm here for you when you're ready to talk.

Call me. Please.
Love-Dylan

Why am I already crying? The tears are flowing down my face onto the pillow below me and I know that this is going to be worse than I thought. I grab the next letter, ready to plow through this, ready to get it over with.

May- It's been a month since you left. I tried to call a few more times but you still don't want to talk. I decided to send you another letter to try to reach you. I miss you, May. I just want to hear your voice and know that you are okay. Please call me back.

I sat on our boulder today for hours and thought of you. To be honest, it's not the same without you. I know I never said anything, but I want you to know that I like you. A lot. More than as my best friend. I like you as a girlfriend and I hope that you will give me a chance to be your boyfriend?

Call me. Please.
Love-Dylan

Oh, no, it's worse than I thought. He wanted to be my boyfriend? I didn't know. I was so stupid.

May- It's been a month and a half since you left. I have to leave to head back to Boulder tomorrow. School starts next week. I'm not ready to leave, I love it here (I know you already know that). I really don't want to go back to school while you aren't talking to me. I tried calling a few more times. Your mom told me to stop calling and that you will call when you are ready.

When will you be ready? Will you talk to me? I'm starting to worry I've done something really bad. Was it the kiss? Was it gross? Did you not like it? I know you're hurt about your parents but why won't you talk to me? I'm sorry if it was bad. I never kissed a girl before and probably need to practice. Plus, I was really nervous. I can get better. If you give me a chance. This is the longest we have ever gone without talking. I hate it. I miss you.

Call me. Please.
Love-Dylan

Oh no. He thought the kiss was bad? He has no idea how wonderful it was. How could I not tell him how great it was?

May- It's been a month since I got back to school. I tried really hard not to call like your mom asked but I can't help it. I miss you so much my chest hurts. Will you ever forgive me? If I knew what would happen, I wouldn't have kissed you. You're my best friend. I don't want to lose you. School sucks. All I think about is getting to next summer and getting back on that mountain and seeing you. You will be there, right? You will come with your mom? I'm starting to worry that I won't ever see you again. That can't happen, right?? Whatever you need from me I will do. I miss you so much, May. You remember my friend Peter from school? He asked me about you and I didn't know what to say.

I messed up. Forgive me. Please.
Love-Dylan

The next letter is a while later—at Christmas time.

May- Merry Christmas. I called your house, but your mom said you didn't want to talk. I don't want to bother you. I just want you to know that I miss you and hope you're okay this Christmas. I can only imagine how hard it is this year with your parents not being together. Do you get to see them both for the holiday or not? Where's your dad? Does he have his own place now?

I think that you must be really mad at me since you refuse to talk to me. I'm so sorry for the kiss, May. I'm so sorry I wasn't good at it, and you don't like me anymore. I hope that you will give me another chance to at least be your friend again. Only five more months and we will be back on the mountain. I can't wait to see you. I miss you so much.

Love-Dylan

My chest heaves. It hurts. *So much*. Why couldn't I just pick up the phone? Why couldn't I just tell him I miss him and that he didn't do anything wrong?

May- It's March 15th. I'm officially 15 years old. I waited all day for you to call. You've never missed a birthday of mine. But it's ten p.m. and I don't think you're going to call me. I had a birthday party at an arcade. You would have liked it. If you would have called, I would've told you all about it.

I don't know why I keep writing you. I think I just miss talking to you. I know you don't want to hear from me anymore but damn this hurts. The summer is almost here and I will be back on the mountain. I asked my mom if she has talked to yours and she said no, but she is sure you will be back to the mountain like you always do, even though your dad might not be coming with. It gave me hope that I will see you again and I will be able to get you to forgive me. I hope that's true.

I miss you. I can't wait to see you.
Love-Dylan

I already know how this story goes, but I still shake as I rip open the next letter.

May- It's May 16th. I waited for you to arrive like I always do. I sat on your front porch and stared out at the driveway listening for the sound of your mom's car. When I heard it, my hands were sweating so bad. It was embarrassing. But only your mom got out. It was only your mom. I didn't have to say anything to her, she just hugged me and said she was sorry. She said you didn't want to come here anymore and that she tried to get you to. I didn't say anything to her, I just went home.

My mom told me that the pain I feel is caused by heartbreak. She said that nothing hurts worse than the first. I think she's right. I think I'm heartbroken. She also keeps apologizing but I don't know why, it's not her fault you won't speak to me anymore.

May- you have to know the truth. The truth is that I love you. I love you so much that I don't really know what to do with myself.

I love this place, my ranch, the mountains, the sunflowers. But somehow, it's not as bright. It just hurts now. To be honest, I may never come back to this boulder or to the sunflower field again. I just don't see the point without you here. I have to find a way to move on but it is so hard.

I will miss you - always.
Love-Dylan

I am in such a hurry to open the next letter; I shred the envelope without any of the finesse I was using.

May- Today is your birthday. This is the first birthday of yours since we met that we have not spent it together. What used to be the best day of the year for me, is now the worst. I won't lie to you, as embarrassing as it is to admit, I spent the day crying. I will probably regret telling you that one day, but I can't help it. I just want you to know how much I miss you. I'm also pretty mad at you. I will never understand what I did that was so wrong. I cannot believe that it would deserve for you to completely drop me from your life without so much as a goodbye.

Even though I'm hurt, and even angry, I just wanted to write to you and tell you happy birthday. No matter what you are doing or where, I hope that it was a great day for you. But even though I want you to be happy, it is time for me to try to let you go.

This is the last time I will write. I won't call you anymore. But if you ever decide to reach out, please do.

Happy birthday, May. I will always love you. I hope one day soon, you will come home.
Dylan
P.S. I hope you like the bracelet I got you. I got it at the mall. It did not cost much but since it has sunflowers, I thought you would like it. You never wear bracelets, but

this is the kind of thing girls like. At least that is what my mom told me so I thought I would try it.

Stuffed inside the letter, tucked into a corner is a tiny bracelet. It has turned a slightly rusty looking color, but I can still see the small sunflowers. My heart stills in my chest. The blood in my veins goes ice cold. With one more letter left to open, I fall asleep, exhausted from the guilt.

Chapter Thirty-Eight

Dylan

The next few weeks are a blur. My days are spent caring for the ranch and my nights are spent tending to my mom. The type of cancer she has is untreatable and so she has known since her diagnosis that she was dying. She finally admitted that she found out in March but did not want to ruin my birthday. Then she was worried that it would ruin my summer with May, so that only furthered her reasons for not telling me.

She has gone downhill fast, and now she is basically bed-ridden. Most of the time she sleeps or reads and watches a little television.

As the hours tick by, my head swims with thoughts of my mom and often of May. I keep trying to think of a way to reach out to her and let her know that I'm sorry and that I want to be her friend, and to see how she is doing and if she needs anything. In reality, I also want to reach out because I need her friendship now, too. I wish I could talk to her about what is going on with my mom, but I know she is busy in treatment. Lynn keeps us posted on how she is while I keep Lynn updated on my mom's worsening condition.

It is now the week before May is to be out of rehab. I know she is headed to stay with her mom and continue outpatient therapy, and I'm so proud of her, but part of me wishes she could be here with me while I go through this. I want to be strong for my mother, but I really could use someone to lean on.

These thoughts rattle around in my head as I hand Mom the painkillers that the doctor prescribes so that she can be comfortable. It is early in the morning and time for her first dose of the day.

She has elected to die at home, so hospice has started to come in daily to assist me with her needs. They should be here around noon.

Watching her wither away before my eyes is draining in the most unreal way. I cannot help but think that I hope this ends soon for her, as her skinny hand reaches for the pills in mine. She never complains, but I know she is in severe pain by the way her jaw clenches tight in the minutes before the meds kick in.

I truly hate seeing her suffer like this.

She does not talk much anymore because she does not have much energy for talking, but today, she is surprisingly chatty as I go to pick up the laundry on the floor.

"Do you remember all of those birthdays of May's we celebrated here? And how they were the same each year?"

"Of course, Mom. How could I forget?" I reach for a fresh set of sheets so that I can remake her bed.

"Have you talked to her since she went to rehab?"

"You know I haven't."

"Have you thought about what I said? About how you need to be her friend?"

"Yes. What're you getting at? You should rest and stop worrying about me and May."

She moves to sit in the chair beside her bed so that I can change the sheets.

"I have a confession to make, Dyl." I stop messing with the sheets and look at her.

"What did you do?"

"Don't be upset with me."

"Okay, just tell me." Little does she know that I am incapable of being upset with her at this point.

"Well . . . you know when Sally went missing?"

"Yeessss?" I say this with the sudden awareness that I

might already know what she is about to say.

"She didn't really go missing."

"Tell me you didn't."

She tries to look innocent as she looks at me with large sunken in eyes. "I did. Sally was tucked away behind the barn. I put her there to hide her from you. I wanted you and May to spend time together alone."

I groan. "Why would you do that, Mom?"

"Dyl, I'm sorry for tricking you, but you two are just so stubborn. You have loved that girl your entire life and I just thought that maybe if you spent some time together, you would remember that."

"It's okay. Don't worry about it. It doesn't matter anymore."

"It's not just the time with Sally, though."

"What? What do you mean, Mom?"

"The fence? Lynn and I needed to force you two together so she came up with the fence idea."

"Lynn was in on it, too?"

"Yes."

"And Candace's parents never asked for a fence?"

"Nope."

"Wow, okay. So, I did manual labor for nothing? I don't even know what to say, but again, it doesn't really matter now."

"But it does. Why haven't you reached out to her?"

"I really don't want to talk about May right now. I'll reach out to her when I'm ready." I finish by fluffing her pillows and take her hand to guide her back to her bed.

"You know, I just talked to Lynn last night and she said she is taking May some stuff tomorrow. It is their last family session. It gave me an idea."

"You really have to stop butting in, I will take care of it."

"Shh. Just listen, Dyl. Why don't you write a letter?

Lynn can take it to her tomorrow."

"How is she going to do that? They're in Vermont."

"Well, we have this incredible thing called the internet. It's great, Dylan. You see, you can write an email and send it to Lynn, and she can print it off and give it to May. Amazing, huh?"

"Okay, smartass." She gives me a small smile as I say this.

"Lynn said if you get it to her by dinnertime tonight, she will get it printed and over to her. Before you fight me on it, just think about it."

"Mom, I wrote her a bunch of letters that she never responded to. I think it would be pretty pathetic if I wrote another one. Besides, I'm not really sure I even know what I want to say to her."

"Dylan, it's not pathetic to care about someone. Just do it. Just tell her the truth. Tell her you still care."

"Okay, Mom, I'll think about it. Why do you care so much if May and I are friends or not, anyway?"

"I don't want to worry about you being alone after I'm gone, Dyl."

"I still have Grandpa."

"Dylan, your grandfather is in his eighties and is too weak to get on a plane or even drive here. He does not have long left, dear."

"He's still able to run the store."

"He sits behind the counter and pays people to run the store."

"Okay, fine, I understand what you're saying. You don't need to worry about me, I'll be okay. I'll make sure of it."

"Of course, I worry, I don't have a choice, you're my son. Please, just write her Dylan. It'll bring me some peace."

Mom's dark eyes dull a bit as she begins to drift to

sleep. She just spent some of her last energy on asking me to write May a letter. It occurs to me that it is the least I can do. I let her fall asleep, slip out the door, and head to my bedroom to grab my computer.

Before I start typing, I brush my hand through my hair and stare at the computer screen. What do I really want to say to May? Obviously, I love her, but with everything going on with her and her treatment, and me having to take care of my mom, I'm not sure telling her that right now would be a good idea. Maybe it's not what she needs to hear. Maybe she just really needs my friendship and not me putting some pressure on her to be more than that. I want to support her, encourage her, be there for her, and forgive her for the past.

With a final nod, I begin to type, knowing now what it is I need to say.

Chapter Thirty-Nine

May

When I wake up from a night of guilt-ridden dreams, it is already the next day and I need to start packing my few belongings. I still have one letter from Dylan left, but it is making me nervous to read it. I can tell it is different than the others as it is in a blank envelope like it wasn't sent through the mail.

At first, I think I won't read it. I have heard enough, I already know the story, but the letter stares at me from the nightstand, threatening to haunt me for the rest of my life if I don't pick it up.

My few belongings are tucked away into my suitcase, my goodbyes are said, so I grab the letter and head for the patio to wait for my mom to arrive.

The sun is sitting low as it is still early. The sycamore trees are just starting to have a hint of color change on the tips of their leaves, as it is now already the middle of August. The quiet breeze is soothing in my lungs, the rustling of the leaves creates a wave of joy that floats through and into my heart. I shut my eyes and reminisce about the mountains and the feel of the breeze on my face.

I grip the last letter in my right hand so tightly that it is creased with worry. Before I lose my nerve, I open the envelope, pull out the piece of paper, and quickly realize it is a printed email. Dylan sent the email to my mom just two days ago.

Lynn- Thank you for printing this and giving it to May. I appreciate it. I hope you are well. Mom loves that you call her so often and check on her. I hope you can get out here one more time before she passes but I suspect it might not be possible because she is fading fast. Thanks again and talk to you soon.

My breath catches in my throat. It sounds like Mrs. Ryder is dying. And soon. Surely, I read this wrong. I make a mental note to check with my mom as soon as she gets here.

May- Here I am again, writing you a letter. I said I would never write you another letter and I meant it. I'm so embarrassed by the other ones. To be honest, the only reason I am now is because my mom really wants me to. Don't get me wrong, I desperately want to talk to you, but I'm not quite sure I'm ready to say all the things I need to say. So, I will start with what I can.
Want to hear something funny? You will never believe it, but my mom lied that day about Sally being missing. She made it up so that we would be forced to spend some time together. I swear she is goofy. I will sure miss her when she is gone. It wasn't just the Sally incident, either. The fence? Your mom and my mom made that up. Candace's parents never asked for that. I know, it's crazy.
I don't know if Lynn has told you that my mom is dying. Terminal cancer. She is in bad shape. Hospice has come in and we have set her up so that she can die at home. It's an aggressive, untreatable cancer so she will be leaving us soon. I'm really going to miss her.
Okay, so hard truth time. I have missed your friendship and need it now more than ever. Another hard truth: I'm sorry. I'm sorry that I was not more forgiving when you asked me to be. I didn't know that you were struggling as

much as you were. Another hard truth: you scared me. I thought I lost you for a minute there. It is crazy how much I still care about you after all these years, but I do. When I saw you lying there on the floor in the wine cellar, I thought my heart stopped beating and would never start again.

I wish I knew everything that happened during those years we were out of touch. The last time I saw you, you were so bright and hopeful and full of life and joy. When I saw you again this summer, I noticed immediately that you were different. You seemed sad. I don't know what's happened May, but I know something must have to make you change so dramatically. I miss you, the real you. I miss the May who smiles constantly, talks about magic, and seeks adventures. I miss that girl and I know she is still inside you, you just lost track of her for a while. I know you will find her again.

I know things suck right now. I know you are going through a lot. I wish I could take away all of that for you, but I can't. I will tell you, though, that I want to be friends with you again. I'm sorry I was mean and have been so hard on you. The truth is, I will always want your friendship, May. You are the best friend I have ever had, and I would give anything to have that back.

When you get out of rehab, and when you are ready, reach out and we will work on building our friendship again. If you never reach out, it's okay. I will understand. I just want you to be happy.

If you ever need anything- anything at all- you know where to find me.

Dylan

I should feel good—great even—about what Dylan writes in this letter, but instead I clutch it to my chest and cry harder than I have over anything else. My hard truth is that I don't want to be friends with Dylan. I want him to love me again. I want everything with him, and I realize that friendship might be the only thing he is willing to give me.

The next week I spend at home getting settled and reassuring both my parents that I'm not suicidal. It is a tough sell as they are understandably overwhelmed with worry. My dad is over almost every day whenever my mom needs to leave the house and I realize they are afraid to leave me alone. I wish I could show them what is in my head. I wish they could see that I want to live and that I finally have something that has been hard for me to find—Hope. Hope for a better day, a better future. One filled with laughter and joy and—if I'm lucky—maybe even a little bit of magic.

Chapter Forty

May

I have read and reread Dylan's letters obsessively—especially the latest one—in the weeks that I get out of rehab.

It takes some thought, but it finally occurs to me how I want to respond.

When he found that tin buried in the back yard, I had stuck it and all its contents into my suitcase for safe keeping. Luckily, my parents kept it in there when they used that same suitcase to gather up some of my stuff in preparation to take me to rehab.

It dawns on me that it might be the perfect start to saying *thank you for saving my life* and *I'm glad you want to be my friend.* It is more than just gratitude and friendship, though. I want to be as brave as Dylan was all those years ago when he poured his heart out to me. He deserves the same from me now.

I pack a small shipping box with the tin inside, that still carries the picture of my parents riding horses with me for my thirteenth birthday, the sunflower I drew and, of course, the letter to Dylan from that last night I was on the ranch.

Then I grab a pen and a piece of paper and write a new letter, one that I hope Dylan will appreciate as much as I appreciate the ones he wrote to me.

Dylan- There are so many things I want to say to you that I don't know where to even start. First, and most importantly, I'm sorry about your mom. To hear that we are losing the great and powerful Mrs. Ryder does things to my heart that can never be undone. If you ever need a shoulder to cry on, support, or anything, you will always have me.

Second, thank you. Thank you for coming to look for me after I left the party, thank you for picking me up and carrying me to the car, thank you for driving me to the hospital, thank you for staying with me until my parents could get there, and thank you for calling my mom to check in constantly. Also, thank you for the letter (and all the letters you ever wrote me).

I have to tell you that what I said that night, about how I had lied and had read your letters and that I thought you were pathetic for writing them, well, that was a lie. I never did read them. Until now. What I didn't know was that my mom had kept them all of these years and she brought them to me while I was in rehab. Please do not be embarrassed by them. They were wonderful and beautiful and painful and just what I needed to hear. Also, I'm so sorry for that night. I didn't mean a word of the hateful stuff I said to you. I regret it more than you know.

You said in your letter that I seem different from when we were kids—sadder. You are right, I have changed. Things have happened that have altered my life and my view on it. I have been working through a lot of difficult stuff in rehab and some are not things that I can really share in a letter, but maybe one day, if you're interested, I can tell you in person. The good news is that I am learning. I'm learning to be happy again, I'm learning to forgive myself for how poorly I have treated myself and those that I love, and I'm learning to embrace life again.

I know how horrible I was to cut you from my life and the way I went about it. I know it was awful of me to never give you an explanation. I wish I could go back in time and <u>slap</u> fourteen-year-old me. You do not need to apologize for anything, by the way. I'm the one who should be apologizing for how I treated you all those years ago and then when you saw me again, I just acted like all that should be forgotten. It is embarrassing how selfish I can be sometimes. It is one of the things that I have learned about myself and that I am working on.

I'm thrilled that you want to be my friend again. I would love that. I have to be honest though (another thing I have learned in therapy), I don't really want to be just friends. I want to be so much more than that. I know that you probably no longer feel the same way about me as you did when you wrote me all those years ago, but I have to try. I have to tell you that I love you. I completely and totally love you. I want to be your best friend, your confident, your lover, your future wife, and baby mama.

I want it all, Dylan, and I want it with you. You might not be expecting this confession, but it's the truth. I know I have spent the last seven years doing everything I can to make you think I don't care about you or that you are not important enough to even say goodbye to. That is the main thing that I want to apologize for, that is the one thing that truly bothers me the *most because it is so far from reality. I want to be clear now, so that you never doubt it again. You are an amazing friend, Dyl, you are loyal, kind, caring, and so damn sweet it hurts. You always took care of me even when we were just small kids.*

If you take away anything from this letter, I want it to be this: <u>if a sunflower was a person, it would be you.</u>

If you are only able to offer me friendship, I understand and accept whole-heartedly. Although, I can't promise that I won't spend my life hoping you will change your mind and want more.

So there, nothing you have ever wrote in a letter to me will ever be as embarrassing as what I just said. So, are we even now? ;)

I love you, Dylan, call me sometime, if you want.

Love, May

P.S. I have put the infamous tin box here with this letter so that you can enjoy its contents. I buried it in the yard the night my parents told me they were getting divorced, just after you and I shared our first kiss which, by the way, is still the best kiss of my entire life, with the one in the tent being a close second. The note I buried in the tin might help shed some light on how I was feeling that night.

P.S.S. Please tell your mom that I love her and miss her terribly. Please tell her that she always made me feel welcome and loved in her home and that she is truly one of the best people I have ever known.

P.S.S.S. Just in case I didn't make it crystal clear: thank you so much for saving my life.

As I seal the letter into one of my mother's interior design work envelopes, it occurs to me that Dr. Wright would be proud.

Chapter Forty-One

Dylan

"Dyl, you have a package out here."

I scurry outside, "Mom, it's starting to get cold out, I think we need to take you back in." I'm always fretting that she is cold, or hungry, or thirsty now. I have officially gone from being the child to the parent and it is the weirdest thing that has ever happened to me.

"I will, but let me watch the sunset first. Something came for you." My mom likes to get outside when she can. Her favorite place in the world is this ranch so I can understand it, but she only has enough energy to be outside for a few minutes at a time.

"Okay, I'll open it in a bit, let's get you inside."

"Dylan, please. The sun will set soon."

"Oh my gosh, fine, Mom. Do you need another blanket?"

"No, I need you to sit by me on this porch swing and open this box that's probably been sitting out here since noon. It rained earlier so hopefully it didn't get ruined."

I have no idea what the package is, nor do I care. I care about making sure my mom is warm and comfortable, but I will indulge her wishes. I pick up the box and slide in under the blanket beside her, careful not to bump her as I do, because I know just how achy her body is.

It's a small box that piques my curiosity since I don't remember ordering anything. The handwriting on the label looks familiar, though.

I rip open the cardboard and as soon as I see the silver color, I know that it is the tin May and I found buried in her yard earlier this summer. I forgot about it until now.

"What is it?"

"I think it's from May."

"*Ohh.*" I ignore the inflection in her tone when she says this. I tuck a letter that is with it into my back pocket and carefully lift the lid to the old tin.

What I find surprises me.

It appears to be a random collection of stuff that May found in her house including an old picture of her riding on Sally, the drawing she did of the sunflowers for her parents one year that I vaguely remember her showing me, and a scratch of paper with something written on it that looks old due to the faded words.

"Read it to me."

I hesitate before reading, "Dylan, today we kissed, and I loved it. But I must leave that kiss, you, and this place buried here in this box. I can't come back here. It hurts too much. My parents have broken up and ruined our happy life. This house, these mountains, and you are stained with their betrayal. I will miss you, Dylan. I will miss your beautiful face and perfect lips. I will miss how funny you are. You are the best friend I have ever had. I love you so much. Forgive me, May."

My breath catches in my throat as the last word escapes my lips. She loved me? She never said that to me before. I didn't know she felt the same way about me as I did her and the reality of it sits in my chest like a bomb.

"Dylan. What was the other thing? A letter she wrote? I'm not going to ask you to read it out loud, I think that is meant to just be between you two. But I will ask that you read it with an open heart."

I nod softly and walk back in the house so that I can let my mom enjoy what I would soon learn would be her last sunset.

I was going to read the letter May wrote me after I went to bed, but I must have fallen asleep instead because it's now three a.m. and her letter is crinkled in my hand.

The soft yellow light of my bedside lamp is flickering slightly. It probably needs a new light bulb.

Whenever I wake up at odd hours of the night, I have the need to sneak into my mother's room and make sure she is still breathing. It's like I am a mother to a newborn baby and the bizarreness of what my life has become does not escape me.

I suspect Mom knows I do this and hopefully it brings her some comfort to know how much I care about her.

I slip off the covers and rake my hand around the back of my neck. The pinch of pain in my body is noticeable as I tense with the contact. I really need to figure out how to relax.

My bare feet hit the floorboards and I tuck May's letter away into the top drawer of my nightstand. I will read it, but I am not sure I have the strength to today.

As I make my way to Mom's room, I listen for the familiar sounds of the television. She usually falls asleep to it. Her door screeches open and I shuffle inside quietly to find the remote.

It is in its usual spot by her left side on the bed, sitting on top of the covers. I reach for it, but something catches my eye before I make contact.

Mom's mouth is ajar in such a way that is painful looking, creaked to the side.

It does not take me long to understand why.

Chapter Forty-Two

May

I get the news on a cold Sunday morning in September.

Mom and I are understandably beside ourselves, but especially my mom. She had just spoken with Mrs. Ryder the night before she died but was busy trying to make dinner, so she cut the conversation short. Now she has this horrible guilty feeling about it.

After calming her down and calling my father, we buy tickets for the next day so that we can attend the funeral. My parents questioned whether I should go—they see me as a fragile person in need of constant protecting now, but I insist on going.

An unspoken urge has formed in my bones.

I must get to Dylan; he needs me right now.

Chapter Forty-Three

Dylan

I spot her immediately.

The crowd is thick with locals from all around town—my mother was well known and quite loved for her barbeque cooking and well-managed ranch. Honestly, every person from this mountain is probably here by my side as I stare at her casket contemplating what the hell I'm going to do now that she's gone.

Grandpa is by my right side, hand on my shoulder. I told him not to come here, but he insisted. He said he couldn't miss his own daughter's funeral, so he paid one of his employees to drive him here. Now in addition to the stress of burying her, I'm stressed about the health of my grandpa.

Mom is buried in a small cemetery with only twenty graves. It's the same place that my father and other ranch owners and their families are buried in. My mom and dad liked this spot because it sits high up on a hill, and you can see almost the entire mountain from here.

My parents bought the ranch when it was going under, back in the eighties from an elderly man who spent his whole life here. He thought my parents were nuts—just some city folk thinking they could manage a ranch but did not have a clue.

As my mom always explained—he was right. My parents did not have a clue as to what they were doing, but they just knew they had to try. After my dad had a stroke, everyone in town thought my mother would sell the ranch and head back to Boulder with me in tow, but she wanted to prove them all wrong and prove them wrong she did. After years of hard work and commitment, she finally earned the respect of every other rancher living on this mountain.

She was one of kind.

This is the running theme of the speeches given by a dozen or so people today who came out to pay their final respects to Mrs. Betty Ryder—ranch owner and woman extraordinaire.

Even with the hundreds of people crowded around this grave, and the sun hidden behind dark gray clouds, and the blurry tear-soaked eyes—I still spot her immediately.

May.

Standing by her parents, dressed in a black pair of slacks and flowy black shirt, and covered in tears, she still manages to be beautiful. For the one and only time today, my heart feels warm.

Several rays of light break through the clouds, setting against several funeral-goers as I gaze over the casket in the direction of May. Something on her wrist catches my eye. I have never known her to wear bracelets. Once, in my heartbroken state, I remember buying her a sunflower bracelet and mailing it to her along with the last letter I wrote, knowing that if she really liked it—liked me, she would wear it. I wonder now as the casket lowers—taking the remaining pieces of my heart with it—if that's the bracelet she is wearing now.

Chapter Forty-Four

May

Everyone leaves the Ryder Ranch at around eight p.m. I never speak to Dylan; I don't get the chance to. He is surrounded by people every second of the day offering him their condolences as he nods quietly. I watch as his grandpa stands beside him the entire time and am taken aback by how much older he looks than the last time I saw him. He looks frail and I wonder if he is unwell. The thought that Dylan might lose him soon, too, forces me to clutch my chest. Even though he is much older, I can still see the resemblance through their large chocolatey eyes, and it makes me smile.

I want to stay behind with him once everyone leaves but my parents will not let me out of their sight, so after a quick hug goodbye, I wave to Dylan and follow my parents off the front porch. I turn back for just a moment, looking for a sign from him—any indication of what he needs from me, but his back is already turned as he steps back into the house.

He is not making this easy for me.

The sun set a while ago and the sky is starless tonight thanks to the cloud coverage looming overhead. My parents are quiet on the trek back as they sink into an awkward place. My parents were alone together for the first time since their divorce when my suicide attempt happened, and now, they find themselves alone together a lot. It must be uncomfortable for them, but they don't complain.

We walk into the house together and I pull the door shut. It seems like odd timing, to ask them what I have always wanted to know, but I never got the courage to in family therapy because those sessions were more about me than them. Suddenly, I have the courage to ask—to ask something that deep down, I think I already know the answer to.

"Mom? Dad?" They both stop in their steps and turn back to look at me.

"What is it, dear?" My mom's voice is low from hours of crying.

"Can I ask you something?"

"Sure." Dad puts his hands in his pockets and nods.

"I know this might sound strange, but I've always wanted to know, and you've never really said, but I think I *need* to know." I am rambling so I stop and take a breath so I can get it out. "Why did you get a divorce?"

"This really isn't the time for that, May." Dad's face tightens more with each word that comes from his mouth.

"Maybe it is, Dave."

"Lynn, we just went to Betty's funeral and emotions are high. How's this a good time?"

"When is it a good time?" I grip the back of the flower-patterned chair and take a deep breath before continuing, "Please, I just want to know. You seemed so in love when I was a kid. It might help me get over it if I understand why."

"May—you have to know that we love you and didn't want to tell you because we didn't want to hurt you. You need to understand that it was a mistake that everyone involved regrets. Please don't think any less of me—or anyone else—because of it." My father's face is contorted in a way I have never see it before.

My knuckles are white, my fingers are aching from straining against the fabric of the chair. I know. I always knew. "Did you have an affair?"

"It wasn't an affair, May. It was one time. But that's all it takes to destroy a marriage."

"With whom?" *Don't say it, don't say it, don't say it.* I

repeat this mantra internally, suddenly wishing I could take back the question.

"Betty. It was Betty."

I grip my hair at the base of my skull and pull as hard as I can while dropping to my knees. A silent cry rips through me, "No!"

It's hours before I stop crying, my pillowcase is soaked and my body aches from shaking. My parents never leave my side as reality sinks into my skin.

I have a lot of questions that they patiently explain, the most important of which is how my mother could forgive Mrs. Ryder and still be friends with her after what happened.

My mother starts by telling me about how she found out—how Betty came by the house one afternoon and was sobbing. How she told my mother that she slept with my dad a couple of nights before and couldn't not tell her. What I didn't know was that my mother did not speak to Mrs. Ryder after that during all the years that I stopped talking to Dylan.

She tells me that after the accident—my first suicide attempt—Betty called her to tell her that she had terminal cancer and hoped to reconcile their friendship and was seeking forgiveness. My mother took it as a sign that she heard from her. A sign that while I worked to improve my life, she needed to work to improve hers, and she had missed her friendship with Betty over the years.

She started talking to her regularly after I arrived on the mountain and they became close again. The one thing they bonded over: getting Dylan and I to reconcile. So, with their renewed friendship, they focused on schemes that would force us to spend time together including the fence and lying about Sally being missing. After hearing my mom explain about Betty, I shift my focus to my dad.

Why?

How could he do this? And with Mrs. Ryder of all people? His shame is obvious as he hangs his head and tries to explain. He says he was a coward and instead of dealing with his recent feelings of unhappiness, he turned his attention to Mrs. Ryder. He says that he wishes he could go back in time and change it, regretting ever losing my mother, emphasizing that it was the worst mistake of his life. He is adamant that he will never forgive himself and misses my mother and our family constantly. As he speaks, my mother's eyes are wide and locked on him.

Then, she surprises us both by quietly saying, "I've missed you, too." My father nods abruptly and places a hand over hers, a desperate look in his eyes.

Mom then turns to me and surprises us both yet again, "I've forgiven Betty for what happened May. I don't blame her for the failure of our marriage, I blame your father, but I also blame myself. We were having problems long before he cheated, and I never did anything about them. What happened was not Betty's fault. It was your father's choice to cheat. I'm so glad I forgave her and we got close again before she passed. May, if I can forgive her, you should be able to," Then with a subtle glance towards my dad, she carefully continues, "and if I can forgive your father, you should be able to, as well."

The three of us hold each other for the next hour and, honestly, it's the best therapy I could have ever asked for.

It's two a.m.

The comforter is tucked up under my chin and I am anxiously staring at the ceiling. I have a lot on my mind, but the one thing that keeps coming to the surface are thoughts of Dylan.

He needs me. I can *feel* it.

I keep trying to figure out what to do. I almost expect him to text me to come over, but he never does. I do not want to text him and be intrusive, but I know deep in my bones that he needs me, so I have to do something. No longer able to help myself, I throw the comforter off me and slide my feet into the slippers I keep right next to the bed. They are soft on the bottom so my footsteps do not make a sound. I think it best to sneak out the window instead of risking the front door. I pull on a hoodie and a pair of jeans as quietly as humanly possible and force my window up just far enough to fit my body through it. It is not as graceful as I would have liked, but it does the trick and before I know it, I can see my breath drifting from my lips in the cold air as I tiptoe toward Dylan's.

The stars have finally come out tonight, the clouds clearing. As I walk briskly along the path to the Ryder ranch, I can see that there is a light on in Dylan's room.

My entire body is shaking with nerves as I walk onto the front steps and reach to open the door, but to my surprise, it is locked. I can't remember a time in my life when Mrs. Ryder ever locked the door to the house and the thought that Dylan might be wanting to be left alone hits me like a brick. The urge to check in on him is overwhelming me so, against my better judgement, I begin climbing the old pine tree that I have climbed so many times before. I am too worried about him to dwell on how humiliating it is to be here doing this again.

The softness of the bottom of my slipper is no match for the scratchy tree branch that I so elegantly scoot across, causing it to fall to the ground below. *Great*, now I will either need to find that shoe or walk back without it. This is beginning to look more and more like a bad idea.

In too deep to give up, I pull myself across the rooftop until I am perched just outside Dylan's window. Luckily, it lifts with ease. I tug aside the curtain and see a soft, flickering light coming from a lamp on the nightstand by his bed. I strain my eyes and make out a figure laying on the bed in the fetal position shaking. It takes a couple of shocking seconds for me to realize it's Dylan and his body is convulsing as he silently cries.

He still has not noticed me yet, or maybe he has, and he is too upset to care. I drop into his bedroom without a hint of grace, hitting the floor hard and no longer caring about being quiet. I push the window shut behind me and crawl into the bed beside him—wrapping my entire body around the back of his trembling one.

I whisper, "It's okay, Dyl. I'm here."

He doesn't say anything but continues to cry.

Chapter Forty-Five

Dylan

I know it's her.

I know it's her when I hear the thud on the roof, I know it's her when I hear the shuffling outside my window, I know it's her when the window is lifted and she drops inside, I know it's her when her body wraps around mine. I know without ever opening my eyes.

I locked the front door after everyone left. It is probably the first time in twenty years that the front door has been locked. I did it out of a moment of sadness and the overwhelming desire to be left alone. I also did it knowing—no *hoping*—that she would find her way inside. I wanted her to work for it—to *fight* for me the way I fought for her all those years ago. My grandpa gave me a knowing nod after I turned the lock, and headed to the guest room. He was tired and knows me well enough to know when I do not want to talk.

When I feel the length of May's body wrap around me, relief washes over like a flood and for the first time since I found her on the wine cellar floor, the weight that had settled onto the center of my chest, lifts just a little.

I do not know how long I have been asleep but when my eyelids flutter open, it's still dark outside and there is that familiar silence that only comes from the night.

I can hear May's soft breathing and feel the warmth of her body under the blanket.

I have never needed her more than I did tonight, and she came through for me—without question. My heart constricts at the thought and further affirms that I am still completely in love with this girl.

I turn over onto my side so that I can watch her sleep. Her mouth is open slightly, her hair is all over the pillow underneath her, and the golden light from my lamp flickers as it casts her face in an iridescent glow.

She is beautiful. Truly and unequivocally beautiful.

With her like this, I can admire her features without judgement. Her nose is tiny and slightly upturned and her lips are curved in the most delicious way. Her eyelashes are long against her cheeks and her long hair looks even more golden in this soft light. I take the chance to glance to her wrist to see if she is in fact wearing the sunflower bracelet. Sure enough, it is the same one that as a heartbroken fifteen-year-old, I had spent hours pondering over before finally dropping it in the mail along with the last shred of hope that I had. I would recognize it anywhere as it would be impossible for me to forget it after how much time I spent staring at it.

As I trace the now rusty edges of the poorly made bracelet on her wrist, I smile. Hope is restored. She does care—she cares a lot.

Somehow, maybe thanks to the energy I'm emitting, she senses me, and blinks awake before I have the chance to look away. I should be embarrassed for being caught watching her sleep, but I'm not.

Before another thought enters my head, my body takes over. I run two of my fingers down the length of her jaw, starting at the base of her ear then settling them on her chin so lightly that she might not even be able to feel it. The way her breath catches in her throat, though, tells me she does.

It is a silent question, one that she answers with a quick nod. I lean over—just enough so that I can reach her and slow enough that she can change her mind.

She doesn't.

Instead, she meets me halfway and—before I can take another breath—her soft lips are on mine.

It is not a passionate kiss or even a sweet, innocent kiss. It is something else entirely—a kiss of comfort. One of need. With its slow caress and warmth, my body awakens for the first time in weeks.

Without breaking contact, I trace my hand down the length of her chest until I reach the hem of her hoodie, then gently run my fingers up and down the skin of her stomach only stopping to dip my fingers along the rim of her pants. She breaks our kiss just long enough to drag the hoodie up and over her head. With her mouth back on mine, I can hear the soft buzz of the zipper of her jeans and with my help, we tug them, along with her underwear, off as she lifts slightly off the bed.

When she settles back down on the bed, completely nude, my heart swells. I take a minute—just one precious minute to steady my breathing and allow the surrealness of what is happening to wash over me in a wave. This moment, lying here with her, before we take that next step, is one that wholly overwhelms me. It's finally happening, she is here, in my bed. To say that I have imagined this a million times over the years would be an understatement. The sad and maybe pathetic truth is that I always think of May, even as I touched another, her face is the one that I would see.

My bones liquify and my limbs tingle at the realization that the moment I have forever wanted, and one I never thought would happen, is unfolding before me. I slide my hand down to my thigh and pinch it just enough to be sure I am—in fact—awake.

By the time my eyes move up her curvy body, skating over the scars on her arm from when she broke it, up past the peak of her breasts and landing on her face, she is looking at me in a way I have never been looked at before. Her face is expressing the same array of shock and awe that I'm feeling. She has waited for this too, maybe even as much as me. With this revelation, something inside me begins to heal as though the very fabric of my cells are stitching themselves back together.

The intensity of her gaze is reassuring and, somehow, even though we have never done this together before, feels familiar.

Unable to waste one more second, I drag my shirt over my head and tug my boxers down quickly, without an ounce of finesse.

We are both lying on our backs with nothing surrounding us now but the air in the room and the sounds of our own rapidly beating hearts.

I slowly turn and lift into position on my elbows with one arm on each side of her head and settle my legs in between her—now open—ones. I dip down into her neck and inhale, relishing in the smell of her skin. She smells just as she always has, like the sun.

I want to savor her completely, spending my time kissing every spot on her body, every freckle, every scar, but I need her so intensely that if I don't sink into her immediately, I fear that my heart will burst from anticipation.

Before I do, I give her lips a soft kiss and ask what I already know the answer to, "Are you sure?" My voice is so low, I almost don't recognize myself.

May takes her hand and places it along my cheek and smiles so wide that I fall in love with her all over again. Then she wraps her legs around my waist and lightly bites my bottom lip.

"God, you're beautiful."

The words rush out of me with force. I have wanted to say them for so long. They are the most honest words I have ever spoken.

A single tear falls out of her left eye, sliding down the side of her face. I'm not worried, though, because I know it's a happy tear. With my heart flying high, and her fingers wrapped into my hair, I push into her, inch by inch, until I am in the only place I have ever wanted to be.

Chapter Forty-Six

May

Buttery soft light drifts in through the cracks in the curtains, running its fingers over the bed.

My eyes blink open, and my body feels liquid-y and warm in the best possible way.

It's a new day. A better day.

I turn my head and find Dylan snoring softly, his bare chest exposed showing off his muscular body. In this light I can *finally* make out what the tattoo on his rib cage is. I delicately touch the outline of a single sunflower. It is curved at the stem as though it is blowing in the breeze. Small orbs of varying shades of yellow are floating around it, seemingly illuminating the flower in drops of sunlight. *Wait—I have seen this before.*

This is no ordinary sunflower. It's for me—for us.

My eyes drift up to Dylan's face, admiring his disheveled dark hair sweeping over his forehead and his still visible dimple.

This man has loved me his entire life. He still loves me—I know he does. The way he held me last night left no doubt in that department. All he has ever done was think about me and my needs. I have hurt him, ridiculously so, and I know that it will take time for those wounds to heal.

One of the many epiphanies I had while in rehab comes back to me as I lay here admiring the beautiful man beside me. My selfishness. I want to be a better person, not just for him, but for everyone I love.

As I lay here, listening to his steady breathing, I think of Mrs. Ryder. One day I will have to tell Dylan about what happened between his mom and my dad, but not today. He does not need to think anything bad about his mom today. She deserves nothing but good thoughts so soon after we lost her. Old May would be furious with Mrs. Ryder. The old May would hold a grudge forever, never forgiving her father or her for what happened, but new May doesn't do that. Instead of being angry, I think of all the things they both have done for me over the years. How kind and welcoming Betty always was and how she made me feel like I was part of the family. I think of how she would stock her kitchen with my favorite snacks and make sure that Dylan was taking care of me.

Mrs. Ryder is so much more than the mistake she made with my dad and my dad is so much more than the mistake he made with Mrs. Ryder. I will not allow that moment to define them just as I will not allow my mistakes to define me. I was angry at both of them right after my parents told me what had happened, but that faded quickly as I recognized how hypocritical I was being. How can I not forgive them for this one mistake when I am so desperately wanting forgiveness for so many of mine?

I sigh a knowing smile, thinking of Dr. Wright's words and how far I have come. Now, I know what I must do, but I need to check with Dylan first—to be sure he understands.

I nudge his shoulder and he wakes easily. As soon as those chocolatey brown and slightly—almost amber—eyes open, he smiles, putting that dimple on full display. I smile back ready to do what I need to do.

"I drew this." My finger is tracing the sunflower on his ribcage.

Dylan blinks a couple of times, but recognition soon follows, along with a smile.

"I thought you spent the last seven years hating me."

His eyes twinkle in the morning sun, "No. I tried to

tell myself that, but obviously that's not true."

"When did you get it?"

"When I was eighteen. I drove back to Boulder and had it done . . . It was in July, on July second to be exact." We stare intensely at each other, the understanding settling between us.

"I need to get my life together." I say this without preamble.

Dylan scrunches his eyebrows together but nods knowingly. "Yes. You do."

"You need to get your life situated now that you have this ranch to run on your own."

"Yes. I do."

"I don't expect you to wait for me. Live your life. If you meet someone else, it will hurt, but it's okay. I owe you a better version of myself and that is what I need to work for. If someone else comes along that makes you happy, I'll understand. I don't want you to wait for me. You deserve better than that. Okay?"

Dylan nods slowly, piecing my words together. He opens his mouth to say something but my fingers on his lips stops him.

"I'm going to live with my mom for a while, maybe get a job. I want to go back to school and get my degree. I have to. I want to."

"You should."

"I love you, Dylan. I don't expect you to say it back. Not yet. I just wanted to make sure you knew."

"I know, May. I read your letter before you got here last night. I know you love me an—"

"No," I interrupt quickly, "don't say anything back. Maybe one day, you can tell me how you feel. But not today."

He smiles again, "Okay. If you insist."

My heart soars as his eyes flicker down over my bare

chest. He reaches for me, pulling me on top of him, so that I'm straddling him.

"We won't talk then." His grin is lopsided and ornery and I cannot help but laugh.

We spend the next hour exploring every inch of each other's bodies, taking our time, memorizing every spot. When it is time for me to leave, I head out the door so that I can get back home to my parents, catch a flight, and tackle my future.

Chapter Forty-Seven

Dylan
Two Months Later

Time has passed by at a rapid pace.

There have been hard times, grief overwhelming me on occasion, but most days are good. I miss my mother, and May, but I'm so busy keeping this ranch going I don't have a lot of free time to be sad about it.

Grandpa never goes back to Boulder. He promotes an employee of his to manager and allows him to run the store. I tell him he does not have to do this, but he insists. I never say it, but I'm so relieved. Having him with me is wonderful, as I was dreading the thought of being here alone so soon after mom was gone.

Managing a ranch on my own is no joke, but I finally have a fulltime ranch hand to help me out. Oddly enough, it is Diego. He lost his job at another ranch a few miles away, and when he called me to ask me if I needed anyone, I was just desperate enough to say yes. It has been good, though, and he is a great help. Luckily, he has not asked me about my status with May, but he doesn't need to. He heard everything that happened the night of her birthday and he knows Candace and I broke up, so I think he just assumes May is mine. Which, of course, she is. What does surprise me is when he brings up an unexpected apology he received shortly after May went back to Vermont after the funeral.

"So, did May tell you she called me? After the funeral?"

I grab a bale of hay and throw it into the stall with Sally. "No, she didn't mention it."

"Yeah, it was crazy cool of her. She called to apologize. She said that as part of her recovery program, she has to call and apologize to everyone she wronged. I guess she felt liked she wronged me."

"Really?" I don't think May ever did anything to Diego that deserved apologizing for, but I keep this to myself.

"Yeah. She said she was sorry for using me. She said she was using me to distract herself from her feelings for you. And maybe to make you a bit jealous. I was so shocked that I didn't know what to say."

I wipe my forehead with the back of my hand, "Wow, she said that? I didn't know she was using you like that."

"Yeah, it's cool, though. She also apologized for how she acted the night of her birthday. I know she doesn't like me enough to date, but I'm glad we can be chill. I always thought she was cool."

"Yeah, she is. She's very cool."

What I want to say is that she is the coolest girl on the face of planet Earth and that I love her so much it hurts, but I don't. The truth is, we have not spoken since she left, and I don't push it because I know she needs to get her life together, and I also know that she is trying to give me space so that I can figure out what I want. If I want her.

What she does not know is that all I'm doing is waiting. Waiting for her to come home, just like I always have.

Chapter Forty-Eight

May
Five Months Later

Today is Dylan's birthday.

I have been strong and not contacted him at all since the funeral, but on a day like today, it feels wrong not to. I wanted to give him—and myself—the space needed to grow and improve.

I have done great. I have maintained sobriety and slowly started to earn my parents trust back. There have been some low points that were challenging for me and for my parents along the way. The main one being when we learned that the man who assaulted me is already serving a forty-year sentence for several other sex crimes he committed in the years after the one on me. The police believe I may had been his first victim, and it began a spree that only ended after the police were able to link his DNA to numerous other unsolved sex assaults throughout Vermont.

Learning this was difficult—painful. I spent several weeks struggling with an intense bout of depression after I learned this information, overcome with guilt. If I had reported him back then, could I have prevented these other incidents? It was only after I reconnected with Dr. Wright and through the support of my parents that I was able to forgive myself for this, too. I have come to accept that the only person responsible for those sexual assaults, is the perpetrator.

After this setback, I continued with my healing by continuing treatment, staying sober, and going through the steps associated with recovery, including the most challenging and agonizing step: apologizing to those I have hurt due to my addiction. I started with my parents, of course, and the hurt my addiction has caused them. They were together when I spoke to them, sitting close, holding hands. I have scarcely allowed my heart the hope that they might get back together again. I never ask them about it, but I hold my breath in anxious anticipation that we might be a family again.

After my first apology, I called and apologized to Diego right away. That one was easy—the tough one was calling Candace.

I messaged her on Instagram and asked her for her phone number. I would have asked for it from Dylan, but I did not want him to know. I did not want to drag him into my mess. She, surprisingly, gave me her phone number and answered when I called.

It was short but easier than I expected. She asked what I wanted, and I told her the truth.

"Candace, I wanted to reach out and tell you that I'm sorry. I'm sorry for how I treated you when I was drinking. I was rude to you, and it was uncalled for. As part of my treatment program, I have to apologize to people I have wronged and so that's what I'm doing. I don't expect forgiveness, but I offer my apologies, anyway."

"Wow. . . I don't know what to say. I don't really care, Miranda, I mean, I've moved on from Dylan, so you can have him. Thanks, but it wasn't necessary."

The line went dead, and I took a sigh of relief.

That was a month ago. I admit I procrastinated a bit on calling her, but at least I did it. As the memory of the call floods my mind, I remind myself that it was never about her. It was about Dylan and today is his birthday.

Feeling brave, I grab my phone and hit call on his name, watching the streetlights from my window dance across my bedroom as I hold my breath. I do not have to wait long because he answers on the second ring.

"May?"

"Hi," I sputter this out before quickly regaining my composure, "Happy birthday, Dylan."

"Heyyyyy." Dylan Ryder has had a few drinks.

"Dyl? Are you okay? Where are you?" I can hear a lot of background noise and maybe some music, so I think he's at a bar. The stab of wishing I was with him hits hard, but I brush it aside, confident we have something worth waiting for.

"I'm at a bar in town. Diego and Jebb took me out, wait, hold on May." He says this with slurring that he manages to make adorable.

After a moment, the background noise quiets down, and I can hear him more clearly. "I'm so sorry, May. I've been drinking. That's not cool with your sobriety, is it?"

"Dylan, you don't have to worry about my drinking. That's my thing to worry about. Are you having a good time?" An insecure part of me wonders if he has a girl and I consider how I can ask him this without seeming overly possessive or weird about it.

"Yesss, but it would be sooo much better if you were with me. I miss you so much, May." The statement hits me with a wave of much needed relief.

"I miss you too, Dyl." How I can utter this sentiment without making it obvious that I'm crying is impossible to say, but I mentally congratulate myself anyway.

"How've you been? How's treatment? I haven't called 'cause I figured you would call me when you were ready." A hiccup. *Man*, I wish I was there to take care of him tonight.

"I've been great, really. I got through all the stuff needed for treatment and, of course, have been sober. But you already knew that didn't you?" I know he has been keeping tabs on me through my mom and it makes me smile to tease him about it.

"Yeeessss . . . Lynn must've told you she talks to me. Is that okay? I just can't not know how you're doin'."

"Yes, it's more than okay, Dylan. But now, I'm ready for you to call me instead. As long as you want to, I mean—unless you're seeing someone?" The words come out quickly and jumbled. I sincerely doubt he would start dating anyone, but I *have* to ask.

Dylan responds with a snort-laugh. "Are you serious?"

"Yes, I mean, it would be okay if you were. I told you that it would be." Lies, I would die.

"May, there's no one else. Never has been. You know that."

I let out a breath I hadn't realized I was holding. "Oh, ok . . . good. I mean, yeah, I can't help it. I don't really want you seeing anyone else, but I'm trying not to be so selfish anymore."

"I don't think it's a bad thing for you to be selfish with me, May. I *want* you to be selfish when it comes to me." Another hiccup. "Are you?"

"Am I what?"

"Seeing anyone?" I smile, *big*.

"No. I'm not. I've just been spending my time getting my life together and missing you every second." It's the truth.

"When're you comin' home? Soon, I hope?"

My heart is beating so hard, I'm sure he can hear it, *hell*, I'm sure people in California can hear it.

"Yes, soon, Dyl. I just finished with my last outpatient treatment session, and I have a couple of classes at the local community college I need to finish before the summer hits. I can be home as soon as they are done—in May. How does that sound?" I'm just being cheeky by referring to coming home in May. It's the month I've always come home, but I know Dylan will appreciate the symbolism of it.

Dylan takes a deep and unsteady breath, "May has always been my favorite month, you know."

Chapter Forty-Nine

May
Two Months Later

It only takes the sound of the car door opening for him to know that I'm here.

I look up to the sound of footsteps and a dog barking to see him standing on the front porch of his beloved ranch.

He is right here in front of me—in the flesh—looking like himself with a simple white t-shirt and his staple muddy boots. He has aged just slightly, the turmoil of what we have gone through this year is visible in the slightly less youthful face of the man I once knew.

His arms are down by his sides and his dimple is in full form thanks to the wide smile stretched across his face.

God, he's beautiful. Even though I have seen his face on my phone screen daily during our calls for the last couple of months, I'm still wholly unprepared for the sight of him.

As I run towards him, arms out in front of me, ready for the embrace, he meets me at the bottom of the steps—prepared to catch me.

I leap up into him, wrapping my arms around his broad shoulders, momentarily stunned that this is really happening and is not just the dream I have been having for months repeating itself.

The warmth and strength of his grip around me as I wrap my legs around his waist and bury my face into the crook of his neck assures me that this moment is very real.

I instantly smell the pine on him, and my heart has never been so full.

He does not need to say a single word to make this moment better but, because this is Dylan Ryder, he does. He always manages to find the right words.

"I'm yours. You know that right, May? Always have been."

Epilogue

May

I'm done with my final test on the final day of class.
I did it.
After two years of community college and two years in the psychology program at the University of Colorado, I am more than ready to walk across that stage to accept my degree and move on to the next step. My plan is graduate school in the fall to specialize in addiction.

My excitement for the future will have to wait, though, because for the next three months, I will be home. It is always hard to be apart from Dylan during the school year, but we get to spend our summers together on the ranch just as we did as kids.

I sprint down the sidewalk toward the quad, looking everywhere for sight of that familiar face.

There he is—in the distance. His smile is big, and his eyes are twinkling when he spots me. To celebrate my final day of classes, he came down to Boulder to stay with me for the week before graduation. I have a small single dorm room that I use during the school year with the tiniest and most uncomfortable bed known to mankind, so Dylan got us a nice hotel room to stay in for the week so we can be more comfortable. He had offered to pay for an apartment while I was in school, but I actually like my little dorm room.

We have a busy summer ahead of us—and a lot of wedding planning. My parents want their ceremony to be at the Ryder ranch, so Dylan and I have a lot of work to do to get the place ready. After spending the last few years taking things slow and going to couples counseling to sort through past hurt, they are thrilled to be getting remarried and starting this new chapter. They even remodeled our old house, and it is now ready for them to start spending their summers there just like they used to.

When I finally reach Dylan, and before I can jump in his arms, he pulls a bouquet of sunflowers out from behind his back. My heart brightens with the gesture, and my body radiates happiness as I pull him in close to me.

To say that we are in love is an understatement. It does not do justice to what we have. We have something so much more. Something magical, something spectacular.

When I was in recovery, I learned a lot about life and about myself. I grew to understand how to cope with past traumas and how important it is to not let them define me. I have allowed myself to heal and to become the person I want to be. Ever since Dylan and I reconnected, I have learned even more—I have learned about love.

I was so naïve and filled with resentment that I convinced myself that love was not real. That it was just a biological construct used to encourage humans to procreate. I thought that because my parents didn't make it, that love must be an illusion. What I did not understand was that even if a relationship ends, it does not mean the love they shared was not real.

With this newfound understanding and with my heart brimming with my love for Dylan, I began to try to answer the question: what is love? To answer this seems insurmountable—an impossible task that artists and philosophers have grappled with for ages. Musicians write songs about it, poets write sonnets about it, even scientists have weighed in—conducting experiments and looking for a specific part of the brain responsible for the sensation of love. I could not tell you what love really is; however, like most of us, I have the desire to *try*.

Instead of unwinding the complicated components of love, such as affection and empathy, I will keep it as basic as possible because I have learned that love really is the simplest of things. Is love tangible? No, of course not. I cannot wrap my hands around the sensation, only the source of what is eliciting the emotion, and it is in that search for something tangible that we lose sight of what love really is. Do not mistake me, despite not being a tangible thing, love *is* real, but it can only be found in the unquantifiable and immaterial.

To me—love is magic. What is magic? Magic is not fairies and mystical beasts or witches or spells like I believed as a child. Magic is what happens when the breeze hits your back as you run through a field of sunflowers with your best friend, their petals wafting perfume all over your body as you fall into a fit of laughter onto the ground. Magic is what happens when the moonlight sails over the face of the person who makes your heart sing. Magic is what happens when drops of sunlight fall to the earth—illuminating your life in its warm glow.

Love is magic, and magic is all around us—you just need to be willing to see it.

Other Books By Kristy Lee

The Worst Thing I Could Do

Glimmers of Hope

About The Author

Kristy Lee was born in Southwestern Colorado. She moved to Illinois after graduating from Alfred University, New York with a Bachelor's Degree in Psychology. Kristy has spent the majority of her career in human resources at various not-for-profits in Illinois and, in 2016, she graduated from the University of Illinois with her Master's Degree in Public Administration. Kristy is now working to obtain her Doctorate of Education in Organization and Leadership.

When she is not writing, working, or furthering her education, Kristy is traveling the globe with her husband, having set a goal of going to one new place each year.

Kristy's debut novel is titled *The Worst Thing I Could Do*. She has since then written *Glimmer's Of Hope and Drops of Sunlight.*

https://kristyleeauthor.com/

www.blossomspringpublishing.com

Made in the USA
Monee, IL
15 June 2022

98050586R00163